OLLIE'S ODYSSEY

WILLIAM JOYCE

OLLIE'S ODYSSEY

MOONBOT books

A CAITLYN DLOUHY BOOK

Atheneum Books for Young Readers · New York London Toronto Sydney New Delhi

Also by WILLIAM JOYCE

THE GUARDIANS
Nicholas St. North and the Battle of the Nightmare King
E. Aster Bunnymund and the Warrior Eggs at the Earth's Core!
Toothiana, Queen of the Tooth Fairy Armies
Sandman and the War of Dreams

THE GUARDIANS OF CHILDHOOD
The Man in the Moon
The Sandman: The Story of Sanderson Mansnoozie
Jack Frost

The Fantastic Flying Books of Mr. Morris Lessmore
The Mischievians
The Numberlys
A Bean, a Stalk and a Boy Named Jack
Billy's Booger

 ATHENEUM BOOKS FOR YOUNG READERS • An imprint of Simon & Schuster Children's Publishing Division • 1230 Avenue of the Americas, New York, New York 10020 • This book is a work of fiction. Any references to historical events, real people, or real places are used fictitiously. Other names, characters, places, and events are products of the author's imagination, and any resemblance to actual events or places or persons, living or dead, is entirely coincidental. • Copyright © 2016 by William Joyce • All rights reserved, including the right of reproduction in whole or in part in any form. • ATHENEUM BOOKS FOR YOUNG READERS is a registered trademark of Simon & Schuster, Inc. • Atheneum logo is a trademark of Simon & Schuster, Inc. • Moonbot and Moonbot Books are registered trademarks of Moonbot Studios LA LLC. • For information about special discounts for bulk purchases, please contact Simon & Schuster Special Sales at 1-866-506-1949 or business@ simonandschuster.com. • The Simon & Schuster Speakers Bureau can bring authors to your live event. For more information or to book an event, contact the Simon & Schuster Speakers Bureau at 1-866-248-3049 or visit our website at www.simonspeakers.com. • Book design by Lauren Rille • The text for this book was set in Adobe Jenson. • The illustrations for this book were rendered in multimedia. • Manufactured in China • 0316 SCP 10 9 8 7 6 5 4 3 2 • CIP data for this book is available from the Library of Congress. • ISBN 978-1-4424-7355-3 • ISBN 978-1-4424-7357-7 (eBook)

To my favorites,
lest we forget

1
Lost and found

When Billy was born he was nearly lost. He came into this world with a small hole in his heart, and for the first few days of his life, he was seldom with his mother and father. He was shuffled from room to room through the maze of hallways that made up the hospital where he was born. The doctors did many tests on Billy, mostly to see how large this hole was and if, as one doctor said, "It was something to be really worried about."

When Billy's mother and father were told about this hole, they were much more than worried. They were afraid in a way they had not felt since they were small children, since before they had learned the words to describe their feelings. But there were no words that could describe or give comfort to the deep unease and desperation they now felt. A new baby is suddenly the dearest thing alive to a mother and father. In one miraculous moment a bond forms that is stronger than any other in life.

Billy has a hole in his heart. Will he be all right? He must *be.* This was all they would allow themselves to think.

So as they sat at the hospital, waiting, waiting, waiting to hear any news, Billy's parents were in a quiet, fearful agony of not knowing. When kids are afraid they hide under the covers, or cry, or scream, "I'm scared!" But grown-ups sit very still and try to act like everything is okay—even if they feel like hiding or crying or screaming, they usually will not. This is a grown-up thing called "coping," which is just a polite way of saying they are terrified.

Billy's father coped by holding his hands together very tightly and clenching his jaw until it ached. And his mother coped by making a small stuffed toy for Billy. "Toy" is a word that feels pleasant in thoughts and memories. But "toy" is also a limited word. Under the right circumstances a toy can become so very much more than something to be played with or amused by.

It can become miraculous.

This toy that Billy's mother was sewing was already special. It was made of various kinds of deliciously comfortable fabric, which she had chosen with great care. And its shape was very pleasing. It looked like a teddy bear, but for reasons that Billy's mother could not explain, she had also given it long ears that were vaguely rabbit-like. So it wasn't really a bear or a rabbit; it was something all its own. It wore a blue-striped hoodie and a red

COLOR #27

B CK of EARS
COLOR
8

COTTON STUFFING

bell

COLOR # 8

COLOR #8

COLOR
#27

BOTTON
of
PAW

OLD
FABRIC
TO WRAP BELL

Color #27

BOTTOM of FEET

SCARF YARN
COLOR
#82

Hoodie
COLOR # 57

BODY of HOODIE
color # 65

scarf around its neck and had a simple, hopeful face that gave the impression of friendliness.

Billy's mother had a keen eye and a mother's instinct to guide her as she made this funny little rabbit toy. Her sewing was expert. This toy may have been homemade, but it didn't look odd or shabby—it looked steadfast and unusually charming. *This is a toy that will matter*, she told herself.

As she sat in the hospital waiting room, trying not to be scared for baby Billy, she was adding a last bit to the toy that would set it apart from any other in the world. She gently sewed into its chest a small heart. The heart was made from a scrap of fabric that came from something very dear to her—a toy *she* had loved as a child. The toy that had been her favorite.

She had called that toy Nina. It was a lovely doll, and the first time she'd ever held it, the name popped into her head and somehow seemed perfect.

Nina had been with her constantly through her childhood, and even when the doll had been loved till it had fallen to shreds, Billy's mom had kept a bit of its once-lovely dress and the tiny bell that had been inside of Nina.

So now these tokens of her own childhood would live on in this toy for her Billy. The bell was inside the heart, and though the blue cotton fabric was packed snugly around it, it gave a faint but pleasant jingle every time the toy was moved.

When Billy's mom made the last stitch, she closed her eyes for a moment as a thousand memories of Nina flooded back to her. But this remembrance was interrupted. She realized the doctor was standing there. He was holding Billy, who was wrapped in blankets and not moving.

For a moment the parents' hearts stopped. But the doctor was smiling at them, and they heard Billy make a yawning sound.

"It's a very small hole," the doctor explained. "A few years ago we wouldn't even have been able to detect it. It should close up on its own. And Billy will never even know he had it."

Billy was okay.

Billy's parents' fear faded away, and before they knew it they were holding him. Billy was tightly clutching one of the toy's ears in his surprisingly strong baby grip. He made a funny little sound:

OLLY OLLY OLLY. And in that instant Billy's parents knew the toy's name: Oliver, Ollie for short.

What they never realized was that another small bit of magic had occurred.

Ollie knew his name too.

2

A New Moon

That night, when they made the journey from the hospital to home, Billy never once loosened his grip on Ollie's ear. The toy dangled and swayed as Billy's mother carried them through the hospital. Billy's father clumsily held bundles of diapers and medicine and towels and baby things that the nurses had given them, and he hovered closely as they walked to the front door. Neither mother nor father could stop smiling at Billy, and they barely looked at anything else. They forgot that Ollie was even there.

When they came to the doors of the hospital, neither noticed that the automatic doors opened for them, or that the night sky was clear and filled with stars, or that a crescent moon shined down upon them. But Billy and Ollie noticed. It was their first time seeing the sky.

As Billy's father helped them into the car he finally looked up. "There's a beautiful moon," he said.

Billy's mother raised her head. "Yes, it is," she said. "A crescent moon."

Billy squeezed Ollie's soft, ocher-colored ear even more tightly. It didn't hurt Ollie. Instead, it made something very important happen, something that only happens when a toy is held by a child for a very long time. As Ollie looked at the sliver of the moon, he thought his first real thought.

It looks like it has a hole in it too, that Moon Thing. I hope it fills up like Billy's.

The bell in his heart jingled just a little as they settled into the car, and the father shut the door.

Ollie didn't know about how the moon changed. There were countless things that Ollie didn't yet understand. A toy's first hours of being new can be very intense. It's as if it is awakening after a long time and learning every aspect of life all over again. Especially a homemade toy. For within their stitching and fabric, bits of their maker's past can be felt or heard like an echo.

So Ollie had a sort of sense of things—of grown-ups and babies and night and day. But he did not really know the words for these things yet. Or what name to give the sentiment he was feeling. So the journey in the car was full of quiet amazements. He noticed much as they drove, and thought many more thoughts and had many questions.

The tall ones are grown-ups. Is Billy a grown-down?

These grown-ups are Billy's parent people. They made him. The mom parent made me. Billy is hers. But I am different.

And then he wondered for the rest of the drive about this difference.

He listened as they came to the place called "home" and they put Billy in the thing called the "crib," and he watched as they quietly turned off the "lights" and then when they "fell" into a place called "sleep." These were all things that he understood almost immediately. They were pieces of the life he would now be a part of. But there were other things he felt but could not put a name to.

There in the crib, Billy held Ollie around the neck, and their faces were just barely touching. Both were soft and warm. Ollie liked soft and warm. He liked the feelings that they gave him. They made him feel a word called "safe." But there was something else he felt, something that was very intense, so he searched and searched in his new toy mind for a word that made it clear to him.

And at last, as the stars and the moon shined down through

the window, Ollie understood how he was different. Billy belonged to his mother and father, but Ollie knew that he belonged to only one person. That was the word he was searching for: "belonged." He belonged to Billy.

And he knew that this word was, for him, most important. It was like a warm blanket that would cover his whole life.

3
The Keeper of Safeness

Billy wanted Ollie with him always and never went to bed without him clutched tightly in his arms. Ollie's head was usually pressed against Billy's chest when he slept, so Ollie listened intently to his friend's heartbeat.

I don't hear a hole, Ollie thought, *but then, I don't know what kind of a sound a hole would make.*

His secret theory was that by keeping his bell heart over Billy's chest at night, he would make the hole go away faster.

It's too bad his heart doesn't have a bell in it, he mused. *Then we'd be just alike.*

And they *were* very much alike, for they were discovering the world together. They were becoming "who they were" together. But while Ollie looked the same and never grew bigger, Billy was always going through something called a "phase," and each of these phases brought many new experiences, which in turn had a different set of words.

First Billy was a "newborn" or an "infant." Ollie didn't understand some of these words, and he was never sure why they came and went, because to Ollie, Billy was just Billy, and as far as he could make out, Billy was simply a "baby."

But whatever they called him, Billy was still soft and warm . . . except when he wasn't. Sometimes Billy was "wet" and sometimes he was "stinky," which Ollie thought was absolutely the right word. (It sounds like what it is.) But he found the idea of "stinky" very odd. *What is up with this "stinky" stuff?* he wondered. *They should get Billy fixed. He leaks a lot. And most of it is stinky.*

Since Billy carried Ollie with him everywhere, when Billy got too stinky it usually meant that Ollie got something called "P.U." Billy's mom would pick Ollie up, hold him close to her nose, and say, "Peeeee yooouuu!" And P.U. always meant "a trip to the wash." Ollie did not like the wash. At all. It was almost the only thing that scared him. It was dark and wet and loud and scary in the wash. And he always had to go through it alone. Billy was never put in the wash. He took a bath.

There were always more changes and more words. Billy became a "toddler" after he began to walk. During this toddler phase Billy usually had one of Ollie's ears clamped in his mouth. This was how Billy preferred to carry Ollie. *I think it helps him toddle better,* decided Ollie, who would forever refer to walking as "toddling." There were certain words that Ollie really liked better than others. For instance:

When Billy was a baby every kiss-like act involved considerable amounts of drool or spit, which the Dad called "slobber." Ollie liked the sound of the word "slobber" more than "kiss."

"Slobber" sounds like, I dunno, ya mean it, he thought. *"Kiss" is okay, but "slobber"? That's the real deal.*

So when it came time for bed, Billy always got a good-night slobber from his parents. Then Mom would tuck Billy in at night, she'd say "Keep him safe, Ollie" before she left the bedroom and turned off the light.

Ollie took this request very seriously. "Safe." Ollie liked the way it sounded. He liked what it meant. He liked the way it made him feel. It was like "soft and warm" but better.

So keeping Billy safe was Ollie's favorite thing to do. He'd put his head on Billy's chest and listen to his heart.

I am Mr. Safe, he'd say to himself. *I am the Keeper of Safeness. The Grand High Safemaster of Planet Billy.*

By the time Billy was no longer a baby but "a little guy," "a fella," or just "a boy" (*Hasn't he always been one?* Ollie wondered), Ollie had also developed a very particular manner of speech that Billy could understand perfectly. A big favorite was "Yum."

This was one of Billy's first words, and he said it whenever he ate something he really liked. Ollie of course never ate anything, but he marveled at food and the effect it had on humans.

Whenever Billy and his dad ate ice cream they would close their eyes and say "YUUUUUUUUMMMMM" in a way that seemed almost alarming. Mom would laugh at them and say, "You guys look so blissed out."

So in Ollie's mind, "yum" was about as good as anything could get.

Then one night, when Billy was barely six years old and was just about to fall asleep after they'd had a particularly full day of bliss and yum and fun, he asked, "Ya know what, Ollie?"

"No. What, Billy?"

"You know what my favorite thing is?"

"Good-night slobbers from your mom and dad?"

"Well, that's pretty close."

"A really yum day when we get to play and stuff?"

"That's pretty close too."

"Then I dunno, Billy."

"My favorite thing in this room, in this house, and in this country and the whole universe of Earth and outer space and everyplace that we don't even know about yet, my favoritest thing is . . ."

"What?!"

Billy looked at Ollie and smiled and said:

"You."

Favorite. That was a very big word.

In the realm of toys, being favorited was a special distinction. It was as yum as it got. There can only be one favorite for any child, and Ollie was Billy's. Ollie felt the same way about Billy. And he now knew a word that fit his feelings better than any other word in the world. *"Favorite" is better than "slobber" and even better than "belong,"* thought Ollie. *It's all those things and more.*

The other toys in Billy's room instantly knew what had happened. They murmured among themselves in awe—"Ollie is a favorite"—over and over. A mysterious cluster of fireflies gathered outside the window, seeming to respond to the news. With a single gust of wind, they vanished.

But there was something else that was listening that night. Something that wasn't a toy, exactly. Or a person. But it hated favorite toys. It sent its helpers to find favorites. It searched for them relentlessly. And because of this something, Ollie would have to be the Grand High Safemaster many times in the days that followed.

4
King ZoZo

Long before Billy was born, and his mother was his age, there was a clown king. In the beginning, Zozo was a happy clown. He had been crafted with great care by a clever inventor who wanted nothing more than to make children happy. And happy they were each and every time Zozo was bonked by balls they had thrown and was knocked backward from his lofty golden pedestal. For every time he fell, bells would ring and lights would blink. And that child was given the wondrous news that he or she could

choose, actually *choose*, a toy from the array of toys that dangled from the ceiling of the Bonk-a-Zozo game.

In those early days Bonk-a-Zozo was the highlight of a little carnival popular with local folks, and Zozo himself was quite handsome, with his high, pointed hat and his starched ruff of a collar and his perfectly fitted suit of velvet. To see Zozo in his heyday, sitting tall and proud on his throne of red and gold, illuminated by globes of light, was much like observing a king upon his throne. A kind and benevolent king who did not mind getting bonked every now and again so that a child might laugh and a toy might find a home.

Because that was the point of Bonk-a-Zozo—the point of Zozo's life, in fact—that these toys, Zozo's toys, find a home, a good home, and within that home, perhaps even have the glorious fortune to be singled out, to be favorited.

In the beginning Zozo never minded that the toys constantly came and went. He never begrudged the others their happiness, their chance of becoming a favorite to one child, because he felt himself to be a favorite to all children—at least to all the children who came to the carnival, anyway.

Zozo felt great pride at being the center of his game. He would always sit tall and straight, waiting patiently for the moment to be bonked.

Being bonked did not hurt, not at first. The balls the inventor used were soft, and often the children missed. Actually, that was the hurtful part in the beginning: when a child missed. Then there would be tears instead of laughter, and a lull of sadness would fall upon the toys at Bonk-a-Zozo.

The inventor was good about giving second chances, though, and later he even installed a clever little button under the counter that he stood behind, a button that made Zozo fall whether or not Zozo had actually been bonked.

Word began to spread among parents and children that when

you went to Bonk-a-Zozo, you would not leave empty-handed. And so Bonk-a-Zozo grew quite popular, and Zozo spent a great deal of time falling and being set right. Each time he fell, the inventor would re-straighten his hat and suit and wipe away any smudges from the clown's smiling face with a soft cloth, saying something like "Good job, Zozo!" And a warmth would flow through Zozo, and a power too, and he couldn't wait to be placed high on his throne once more so that he could continue to do a "good job."

It was during this golden period of Zozo's life that a new toy was brought to Bonk-a-Zozo by the inventor. The new toy was a doll; a dancer, to be exact.

What Zozo first noticed about the dancer was her posture. Most toys slumped a little—they couldn't help it, of course, being mostly plush stuffed toys as they were. But the dancer stood exceptionally straight with one arm arched gracefully over

her head, and her legs very close together and her toes pointed. She wore bright-red dance shoes and a blue skirt that puffed out around her waist.

Her hair was dark and up in a neat bun at the top of her head. Her face was painted on like Zozo's, but the painter had used a far more delicate touch. The dancer's eyes were glued on and fringed with long curling lashes, and her straight thin nose was in perfect proportion to the serene curve of her mouth. And whenever the wind blew a little and the dancer swayed, there was a quiet jingle of a bell. Zozo could not see it, but he believed it was inside her, in the place where her heart would be. And Zozo cherished the sound of that bell, for in it he heard a music unlike any he had ever heard—a song that seemed only for him.

Over time Zozo came to admire the dancer greatly, but always from afar. He never became too friendly with any of the toys in the Bonk-a-Zozo, even after hours when the children went away and the carnival was dark. Zozo was more or less a king after all, and as a king, he had a certain dignity and distance to maintain. At least that's what the toys believed.

Also, Zozo was sure that the dancer would be claimed quickly, and then she would be gone so there was no point in being friendly. The dancer was far too beautiful to remain in the Bonk-a-Zozo for long.

However, the dancer did remain. The inventor had hung her behind the other toys at an angle no child could see. And he had set her so she faced Zozo, not outward toward the midway.

She was the only toy who had ever faced Zozo.

At first Zozo worried that the dancer was sad about being overlooked time and time again. But she never *seemed* sad. Her expression never changed. And gradually, over the years, Zozo felt a connection growing between them, something unspoken and fine, like a golden thread linking them together. He took great comfort in seeing the dancer day after day as the seasons came and went.

In time the dancer became all Zozo thought about or focused on. He did not notice when things began to change at the carnival. He did not notice the crowds growing thinner, the line at the Bonk-a-Zozo getting shorter. He did not notice that some of the rides had closed around his booth, that several signs had gone up saying UNDER REPAIR, and that still, no repairmen ever arrived so the signs were never taken down.

Zozo *did* notice when one day the inventor did not return. The inventor had always left for the night, but he had always come back. Then one morning he did not.

For days no one came to open the Bonk-a-Zozo booth. The toys were uncertain and afraid. There was much chatter and worry among them. "Are we closed? Will we be thrown away?" they asked one another. The dancer spoke up.

"All will be well," she assured them. "Zozo will find a way."

This quieted the toys. They swiveled to peer at Zozo on his throne. Zozo was deeply happy to hear the dancer's faith in him. He smiled as best he could and nodded. "Yes," he told them. "I will find a way." And so the toys calmed and were no longer scared. But that night Zozo worried. *They believe in me*, he thought. *I must find a way*. But what could he do?

Belief is a powerful thing. It can bring about extraordinary changes. For Zozo the toys' belief grew and burned inside him until he had something toys rarely ever have: a heart.

At first Zozo didn't know what had happened to him. He felt so strange. He knew he was somehow different. When he looked up at the dancer and she looked back at him, he felt a joy more intense than he had ever known. But he also had feelings that he did not like at all. Try as he might he was not able to do anything to help the toys. He could not move on his own. He could not speak in a way that any human could hear. All he could do was hope. *Something must happen*, he thought. *If I cannot make something happen, then why am I here? Why do the toys believe in me?* Days went by and nothing changed, and yet, the toys continued to have faith in him.

Zozo's joy began to shrivel. It shriveled until it became something else: a deep, humiliating shame. He knew he was failing the other toys, and this awful understanding simmered inside him, dimming his hopeful heart.

After more days than the toys could count, someone did come, but it was not the inventor. It was a man Zozo had never seen before. Though he reopened the booth, this man did not smile at the children when they arrived. And though he knew about the secret button under the counter that made Zozo fall backward when he wasn't hit hard enough, the man did not give any second chances.

"No wonder this place wasn't making any money," the man had grumbled. "The old man's practically been giving the toys away."

Word began to spread among parents and children that Bonk-a-Zozo was not as easy as it used to be. For a while children still lined up; they still tried to get a toy. But now they nearly always went away empty-handed. The stuffed animals grew dusty and stopped caring whether they slumped or not. On the rare occasions when a child did win a toy, the man never replaced it with another. In time there were so few toys left that the dancer was now in plain view.

Slowly the man made other changes too. He moved Zozo back even farther from the counter. He replaced the soft balls with hard ones. Now when Zozo was bonked—which wasn't so often anymore, but still happened occasionally—the bonk was not a gentle one. The bonk chipped some of the paint off Zozo's face. It dirtied his velvet suit. It made the ruff tilt to one side and the hat bend at an odd angle.

Soon the line dwindled to nearly nothing at Bonk-a-Zozo. Days would pass, sometimes weeks, without a single customer. And after a while the customers weren't young children anymore, but older-looking ones or even adults who sneered at Zozo and laughed at his dirty suit and crumpled hat.

Somehow the carnival remained open even though hardly anyone ever came. The Bonk-a-Zozo booth began to sag on one side. The paint peeled. An even thicker coat of dust settled over everything. The few toys who were still there no longer talked among themselves, and Zozo felt they no longer believed in him or in anything at all. They had become hopeless.

But Zozo remained sitting on his throne. What else could he do? His only consolation was the dancer. At least she was still there, still standing directly across from him, gazing at him with her lovely eyes and serene smile. The fine golden thread still linked them together. She was the only thing who kept the light of Zozo's heart burning. She stood there and silently reminded Zozo of his glory days, of the time when his suit had been clean, when his ruff had been starched. She reminded him of a time when children and grown-ups alike laughed with joy, not with bitterness. He could feel that she still believed in him.

One day a family came to the park. The father had visited the carnival as a child and wanted to now show it to his own daughter. But of course nothing was as he remembered, and the family was just about to leave when the little girl stopped right in front of the Bonk-a-Zozo.

"Oh, Daddy, look at that dancer! She's so pretty! Can we try to get her, please, please, can we?"

A pain hit Zozo deep in his heart. He was startled by the pain, and he looked at the dancer, and she looked back at him. If she was taken, if the golden thread between them was cut, he did not know what he would do.

Still, it had been a long time since a child had won a toy, any toy. Why should this little girl be any different?

As the child picked up the ball, Zozo let his gaze drift away from the dancer, and he focused on a point far off over the child's head, as he always did. He sat straight and tall as ever, and he waited.

The first ball missed, of course. And so did the second.

The third ball, however, did not miss. It hit Zozo right in his chest, right over his heart.

It was as if a bolt of lightning had blistered Zozo's soul and knocked him backward. And by the time his mechanics brought him back upright again, he was numb and desperate. He heard the little girl laughing with joy. And he also heard the jingling of the dancer's bell.

"You will be my favorite toy," he heard her say. "And I will call you Nina."

It seemed to take forever for his throne to rotate back in place. As it did Zozo saw that the dancer was no longer in her spot. He could see the small hook from which she had hung; it still had a shine to it, unlike the other rusted hooks that had been toy-less for so long. There was a tiny piece of ribbon from her dress still wrapped around the hook, and it rippled in the chilly breeze. Zozo could not accept what he was seeing. But he could hear the almost rhythmic sound of the dancer's bell growing fainter.

His pedestal gears clicked his platform into place just in time for him to see that the girl was clutching the dancer with both hands. They were already walking away.

The dancer's face was barely visible above the girl's shoulder. Zozo could see her bright beautiful eyes. He could hear every step the little girl took for it shook the doll's bell. Then the family

rounded the corner of the midway and were out of sight. Gone. He could hear the bell no more.

The golden thread was broken.

Nothing mattered to Zozo after that. Not the feel of the balls hitting him. Not the dirt on his face or the rips in his costume.

It did not matter when more and more signs saying UNDER REPAIR were posted. Nothing was ever going to be repaired at the carnival; nothing was ever going to be fixed. Zozo knew that now.

It did not matter that the man stopped showing up for days on end, that he stopped showing up altogether. It did not matter that the carnival closed for good and the booth was abandoned.

It did not matter that the hot sun baked Zozo's painted and cracked face, or when the cold winds blew or the hard rains pelted him. It did not matter that the Earth itself began to slowly melt and sink, pulling Zozo down, down into the darkness.

5

an awfully huge a-venture

for Billy and Ollie, nothing really changed after the night Ollie had officially been made a favorite—except that life got even more yum.

All day long there were forts to build and trees to climb and bikes to ride and games to make up. Billy and Ollie lived most of their time in made-up adventures. Sometimes the couch was made of rocks, and the carpet was a sea of lava, and they had to make their way to the kitchen by stepping on chair cushions to avoid being melted. Sometimes they were bumblebees and buzzed and hovered everywhere making a *bzzzzzzzzz* sound and stinging the car. It didn't matter if it was rainy and they were inside, or if it was sunny and they were out. All that mattered, from morning to night, was that Billy and Ollie were always together, never apart.

When Billy was small he would simply grab Ollie by an arm or leg or ear—whichever was handiest at the moment—and carry him from place to place. As Billy grew bigger, however, his parents gave him a backpack, and that backpack happened to be the perfect size for carrying Ollie around on an A-venture. This was Billy's way of saying "adventure." So when he would say to Ollie, "I believe we need to go on a huge A-venture," the toy always knew what he meant.

An A-venture could involve something with Billy's mother and father, like going to the zoo or a baseball game or even just

the grocery store. But an A-venture could also be something for just the two of them—Billy and Ollie, alone together. These were called "huge A-ventures."

A huge A-venture could be a trek through the tallest mountains in the world, a place so remote only a tribe of fierce abominable snow-men dared call it home. (This was the hill in the front yard down the street.) A huge A-venture could be a voyage across dangerous distant seas (this was usually across the living room carpet, which was ocean blue) in pursuit of a band of pirates and a chest of stolen gold. A huge A-venture could be a trip to the moon via a rocket ship (really a refrigerator box), which sat in the backyard.

There were a few rules about huge A-ventures, but they were grown-up rules. If Billy and Ollie were on their own, they always had to let the parents know if they were leaving the house, and later, as Billy got older, the yard. A lot of times conversations would go like this:

Billy: Just wanted to let you know that Ollie and I are going to toddle to the moon today.

Mom: Sure, honey, that's fine. You'll be leaving the yard, then?

Billy: Prob'ly.

Mom [To Billy]: Okay, Billy, just remember the rules. [To Ollie]: And Ollie, remember to keep Billy safe.

Ollie: Tell the Mom "ditto."

Billy: Ollie says "ditto," Mom.

Neither Billy nor Ollie knew what a "ditto" was, but Billy's father often said it when he seemed to agree with something. And they both liked the sound of it. So "ditto" was their way of saying yes with deep enthusiasm.

———————

Leaving the yard meant following the Number One Big Rule: Never Cross the Street Without an Up (which was short for "grown-up").

This was big. It was a "deal breaker," as Billy's mother and father put it. It was "bad news." And it was also "highly illegal." As far as Billy and Ollie could tell, anything that was against the rules was "illegal." And there were many "illegals." Cookies before dinner were "illegal." Not brushing your teeth before bed was "illegal." And crossing the street alone seemed to be "super illegal," which could lead to the thing they feared the most: "being in trouble." Trouble was a place they never wanted to be near. You could be standing around without a care in the world, and suddenly you would be in trouble for something you maybe even forgot you'd done.

You were then surrounded by a cloud of "bummer." And it

felt terrible. And you didn't know what would happen, but it wasn't going to be good, because your parents are "mad at you," and when they are "mad at you," it is not at all fun. It was the total absence of fun. It was frowns and "go to your room" and "you can't play," and nobody talks and you don't know when it will be over. And you start thinking about Hansel and Gretel and running away or being lost in the woods or trapped by scary old ladies and eaten or turned into frogs or just lost from all happy tuck-ins and kisses good night and all the world's yum.

Once "in trouble," it seemed to take forever to get out of it. Trouble time went 50 times slower than regular time and 377 times slower than fun time, which went faster than any other time. Which is very strange and unfair and extremely true. But being in trouble would always pass, and the world would be bright again and there would be smiles and going-outs and plays and have-funs.

But the memory of being in trouble kept Billy and Ollie very aware of doing what they were told, which wasn't a problem, except when their ball happened to roll into the street. Then it took an extra second for Billy to remind his feet not to leave the sidewalk, but to wait at the edge of the curb for a neighbor or some other Up to throw the ball back.

Sometimes Billy and Ollie would be standing there, waiting for a ball to be thrown back, and they would speculate on what would happen if they even let one toe of one foot drift from the curb.

"There's prob'ly an alarm," Billy would say.

"And the police would come," said Ollie.

"And they'd lock us up in the jail."

"Yeah."

"And throw away a key."

There would be a pause, and then Ollie would say, "Sounds a lot like being in trouble."

"Yeah."

Luckily, Billy and Ollie only had to cross a single street in order to get to their favorite place: the park. And there was a nice man called a Cross Guard who made sure that Billy and Ollie made it across the street safely. Cross Guard's real name was Mr. Beasley, and Billy just called him Mr. B.

The park was at the end of the block, and it had massive old trees (bigger than the trees in Billy's yard) and a playground. The two of them wondered a lot about the word "playground."

"Are there other kinds of ground?" Ollie asked.

"Gotta be," replied Billy. "Bummer ground, where bummers happen . . ."

"Wow," said Ollie.

"And how wow," said Billy.

With bridges and tunnels and ropes and swings and monkey bars and a slide, the park was a place for many huge A-ventures.

It had other kids as well, which was great, and Billy and Ollie had lots of friends there. There was Hannah of the Runny Nose, who was very nice and always had at least one nostril clogged. She could even blow booger bubbles when asked, which made her almost enchanted to Billy and Ollie. And there was Perry, who had many freckles and was very good at making things up and sharing any good sticks he found. And there was Butch, who had a very short haircut and preferred muddy places, which was fun, but he would sometimes act nice and then "commit mean," then afterward say he was sorry, it was an accident, even though it wasn't. Most of the time Billy and Ollie preferred to play alone, just the two of them, because Ollie, like all favorites, instantly and completely understood Billy so that when Billy would suddenly say "Ninjas—in the bushes," Ollie would immediately respond with "Gotcha covered," and they would be lost in a game with rules that didn't need any explaining.

Sometimes Billy's parents came to the park with Billy and Ollie, but more often as Billy got bigger, they didn't. And that was okay. There were always other parents or friendly neighbors around, always on the lookout for anything amiss, so Billy was totally safe when he was at the park.

But the park was no longer safe for Ollie. Not since he had been favorited. Billy and Ollie didn't know it yet, but they were being watched. Watched by beings who did many illegals and were not nice, who committed mean very often, and came from grounds that had once been for play but were now dark and cruel and unforgiving.

Billy and Ollie were about to be in a kind of trouble much worse than any they had ever known.

6
the creeps

The Creeps had been watching Ollie even before he had been named a favorite. They had suspected that he would become a "fave." And the park was where the Creeps intended to toynap Ollie. The Creeps were stunted, scroungy creatures assembled from faded and rusty bits of machines, wires, garbage, and torn-up toys. They weren't much larger than kittens, but they more than lived up to their name: they were deeply creepy, indeed.

The Creeps usually went on their missions in units of five, and each Creep had a specific task.

Creep 1 kept a constant eye on the favorited toy. They were missioned to "secure and deliver" any favorite toy, which in Creep speak was called "a Fave."

Creep 2 was always on the lookout for anyone or anything that might see them. Dogs were a major problem. Unlike adult humans, dogs paid close attention to the world around them. If a dog heard, or saw, or smelled the Creeps and came to investigate, Creep 2 would whisper "Ruff-Ruff coming!" and they'd get ready to run and hide, or drive the dog away with tiny stink bombs, which every Creep carried for defense.

Creeps 3 and 4 were in charge of capturing and carrying away the Fave. They were armed with a variety of nets, hooks, and strings for binding.

Creep 5 was the leader and was called "the Super Creep" or just "the Super."

The Creeps were extremely good at blending in. They always traveled in shady parts of yards and parks, or in street drains and pipes. If they ever came close to being seen by a human, they would collapse on the ground and lie very still. To anyone who noticed, they looked just like little clutters of trash.

Billy and Ollie were totally oblivious to the Creeps. They had no idea that every time they left the house, the Creeps were following them. They had no idea that when they went to the park, the Creeps stealthily watched their every move. And when Billy and Ollie settled into a good game, the Creeps were never very far away, spying and plotting.

And so it was that on this particular day Billy had decided the swing sets would be a good place to start their huge A-venture. Ollie was hanging out of Billy's backpack as they swung. They were in dinosaur times. Billy and Ollie were pterodactyls swooping through prehistoric skies. Just a couple of trees away, in a bank

Super Creep

of thick shrubs, the Creeps were keenly observing. They spoke in gargly whispers:

Creep 1: Now they swing on the sets. the Billy boy has the fave in a pack-'n-the-back-back-back.

Creep 3: We can shoot down from the tree limb low, the limb 'bove the swing.

Creep 4: Yeah! And share the pack-'n-the-back! pull it up and take the fave already inside!

Super Creep: Don't be a dip! too many ways to get glimpsed! there's mummies and dads by the skads. they'd be freakin' and screamin' and chasin' and grabbin' at us in half a dash.

Creep 2: The Super is right. we got parentals front, back, and both sides. and six Ruff-Ruffs. two on leash and four roamin'.

Super Creep: See! not enough stink bombs to deal with that pack, so we keep watchin'. we takes some time. plays it SMART. then nab the Fave and makes our way back to the boss, quick as whistlin'.

The other four Creeps nodded in agreement and settled in. It might take days, even weeks, but stealing favorites was what they did. And they were good at it. Their boss would accept nothing less.

7

an old friend

Once the carnival ground began to sink, Zozo lived for some years in a topsy-turvy version of his old home: an underground maze of drainage tunnels that had been beneath the grounds of the amusement park. Many of the old booths and rides had washed down and settled in these damp, dark tunnels.

This vast underground world was a sad, haunted space. Zozo's heart, which he'd grown so many years before when his fellow toys had believed in him, was now broken. When he lost the dancer, he was so filled with hurt that though he could, like all toys, move when no one was looking, he lay moldering for months in the wet, mildewing wreckage of his old booth, never so much as blinking, for his sorrow left him as blank and lifeless as a plank of wood.

But then his sorrow began to decay into something else, something worse. Anger simmered. Then hate—first a flicker—began to burn. He thought over and over of the last words the little girl had said to the dancer as she took her away: *You will be my favorite.* Those words charred deeper into his darkening soul. Then he thought of a way to avenge his hurt, and that is when Zozo finally stirred.

Slowly, over time, Zozo assembled a warped and mournful world of fun-house mirrors, snarls of roller coaster track, giant teacups and swan seats—all sheared from their rides, grounded forever. This place, located at the center of all the drainpipes, became a kind of laboratory where Zozo began to work his vengeance.

He had always been a keen observer. Through the years he had watched the inventor who had made him tinker with various machines and gadgets. Zozo had learned much in those years, and now he poured that knowledge into an increasingly elaborate plan. For after he'd completed his underground world, he began to create its inhabitants.

An army! He built an army of small creatures, cobbled together from the crumbling leftover toys of the Bonk-a-Zozo game, and bits of wire and metal and rags. Each was given a drop of the rust and oil, the foul liquid that corroded inside his mechanical workings that seeped from his chest. These creatures soon forgot their innocent toy beginnings and became things of ill will and mean spirit, a vast regiment of small but

efficient mercenaries he christened "the Creeps," who he meticu-
lously trained and then sent out into the human world with
very specific orders—to bring back what Zozo could not abide:
favorite toys.

8
Cool, we're going to a wedding! What's a wedding?

Of all the huge A-ventures Billy and Ollie have had, the Wedding was shaping up to be the scariest yet.

At first it sounded great. It was a party, and there would be a gigantic cake. That was all Billy needed to hear. But then his parents began to explain all the things that he'd "have to."

You have to "dress up." Not in a costume, like on Halloween—that would have definitely been fun—but no. For the Wedding you have to "put on a Suit." Dad occasionally wore a suit, and Billy never thought it looked very comfortable. Or fun. Just . . . grown-up. So Billy had to go to a store and "try on" about ten different suits. There were other kids at the store, and none of them liked this whole business of going into a "dressing room" and changing—getting undressed and dressed and coming out and having the salesperson say, "Oh, that looks adorable," no matter how stupid the suit looked.

Ollie stayed in Billy's backpack for all of this, but he was watching and wondering what this weirdness meant. A suit actually had several different parts to it: pants, of course, but also a jacket and a thing like a jacket that had no arms, called a vest. Plus, you have to wear a superclean white shirt that had to stay tucked into the pants, and black socks.

When they got home from the store, Billy and Ollie sat on Billy's bed and looked at all the pieces of this suit.

"I kind of like this skinny scarf thing," said Ollie. "It looks like my scarf, just fancy-nicer."

"They call it a Tie," said Billy, who then flung it around his neck just like it was a scarf. "But it's better as a scarf."

"Yeeeep," said Ollie. "Plus, you look like me when you do that!"

"Yep!" said Billy, and he grabbed Ollie and held him out like he was flying. Then Billy ran through the house making airplane sounds until his mom made him stop and put the Tie away because it was "not a toy." After that, Billy hated the Tie.

"Do I really have to wear the Tie?" Billy asked his mom for about the hundredth time on the morning of the Wedding.

"Yes," his mom answered patiently.

"Why?"

"Because it's what boys wear to a wedding."

"Why?"

"Because you're supposed to dress up."

"Why?"

"Because it's a special occasion. And"—Billy's mom quickly

continued before her son could get in another "why"—"because you look so handsome!" And she kissed his cheek.

Billy scowled. He didn't think he looked handsome. He thought he looked like an alien. Billy but not Billy. Especially after his mom combed his hair over to one side—he never wore it that way—and after he crammed his feet into the Nice Shoes, which were so very Not Nice but MISERABLE IN EVERY WAY. They were hard—no, almost impossible—to put on. Once Billy was finally able to get his feet into them, his "nice socks" were all pushed up at the heels, and this made his toes scrunch up. The shoes themselves were as heavy and unbendable as concrete. And they were hot. And they hurt. And Billy despised them.

"I can't even run in these," Billy complained to Ollie.

"I guess that's the point," Ollie replied.

"Yeah, I guess you're right," Billy admitted. Because it was true that his parents had already warned him that there would be No Running, No Playing, No Shouting whatsoever at the Wedding. Billy would have to sit quietly for a long, long time, and even when he didn't have to be totally quiet anymore, he would still have to be on his best behavior, which definitely meant No Running. *This wedding cake sure better be GREAT*, thought Billy.

The absolute worst thing about the Wedding, though—beyond the Suit and the Nice Shoes and the No Running—was that for some reason Billy's parents wanted him to leave Ollie at home.

"Why would I leave Ollie at home?" Billy asked in surprise.

"Well, weddings are a grown-up thing," Billy's mom explained.

"And you're getting to be so grown-up yourself," Billy's dad added. "Maybe it's time to give Ollie a break and leave him at home."

Billy looked at Ollie, and Ollie looked back. But neither said a word until after the parents had left the room to finish getting dressed themselves.

"I won't go on any huge A-ventures without you, especially not to some stupid wedding," Billy grumbled.

Ollie didn't respond at first. What Billy's mom and dad said had confused him.

"Why do they think I need a break?" Ollie asked finally.

From the years he had been with Billy, he knew that a break didn't actually mean breaking him in two, which would be hard to do, since he was a plush toy. He knew a break meant something like a nap or a time-out. But usually Ollie only did these things when Billy did them.

"I don't know," Billy said with a sigh. "I guess it's because I'm getting older."

"So?"

"So, when you get older, I guess you leave your toys at home sometimes."

"Why would you do that?" Ollie asked, his turn to be surprised.

"I dunno," Billy said in a quiet voice. "But I never see any grown-ups with toys."

"Yer right," said Ollie.

"And everybody grows up," said Billy, even more quietly. They both sat in confused silence for what seemed like the slowest time they had ever felt.

"Where are your parents' toys?" The question just popped out. It suddenly occurred to Ollie that he'd never seen even one of Billy's parents' toys except in photographs in the Photo Album, which was this big fat book with little square pictures that were pasted onto heavy black pages. At the front of the album book, the pictures were from olden times, when cars looked funny and different and everybody wore nutty clothes. These people in this part of the book were called grands and greats and cousins and stuff, but Ollie hadn't met many of them. On one of these pages was a picture of Billy's mom when she was a kid. And this picture was very strange because in it the kid of Mom looked sorta like Billy and sort of like the GROWN-UP of Mom. And this really confused Ollie. That a kid would become this other thing. A GROWN-UP.

And Billy couldn't really figure it out either. He just knew that it happened on a "someday" that was a long, long time from now. And he would be getting bigger every day and then finally he wouldn't get any taller and that was kind of when he would be done upping his growth, and therefore be GROWN UP.

But there, in this picture of his mom from back in her kid days, she was holding a toy. A doll. A dancer. Her name was Nina. Mom always said she loved Nina to pieces. And if Billy asked where the doll was, she would point to her chest and say, "Right here."

"I don't know where their toys went," Billy admitted, answering Ollie's question at last.

"So what happened to them?"

"I don't know," Billy said again, frowning. "It's kinda like they go invisible. Or just go away . . . I mean, I don't think Dad remembers his toys."

Ollie was so shocked, he could not say another word. Finally, Billy broke the silence.

"I'll never forget you, Ollie," he said, bringing his favorite close. "No matter how grown-up I get."

"Promise?" Ollie whispered.

"Promise," Billy replied.

But Ollie felt like the security of his blanket called "belonging" had just been torn apart.

9

A MILLION GAZILLION PEOPLE

After that conversation Billy was determined. He would not go anywhere without Ollie, especially not to the Wedding.

Billy prepared his Getting to Bring Ollie to the Wedding speech with considerable skill. He had put Ollie in his backpack, which was on his shoulder. So when his parents were standing at the front door—ready to leave and saying loudly, "Come on, Billy. Let's go! We're going to be late!"—Billy walked toward them and began his "explaineration."

He talked very fast. "I have to bring Ollie 'cause he really wants to see a wedding and he'd be too lonely if we left him here and I've got him in my backpack, which I need to bring anyway because I just wanna bring home a hunk of the giant wedding cake and no one will see Ollie or anything and it'll help me stay still and not run and all the other 'nots' I'm not supposed to do at this Wedding. . . ."

Billy hadn't even finished and his parents had given up and opened the door and were walking him toward the car. Billy didn't understand many things about grown-ups, but he had developed a sense of how his parents would respond in certain situations. For instance, when they were in a hurry, it was much easier for Billy to get his way if he explained to them exactly why he wanted to do something they did not want him to do. Crying to get his way made his parents cranky. Yelling made them angry. But explaining seemed to confuse them, and it took time, which, when you're a grown-up in a hurry, is the one thing you don't want to have taken.

As they drove to the Wedding, his parents made Billy promise to keep Ollie safe inside the backpack at all times. They said that since he was older now, it was Billy's responsibility to keep track of the backpack so that Ollie would not get lost.

Billy agreed to all the terms just as they pulled up at the Wedding.

"Victory, Ollie," whispered Billy.

"Ditto," Ollie whispered back.

When they got to the Wedding, it was a little overwhelming because there were so many people, and Billy wanted to run and jump and shout immediately because it felt like his whole body was going to explode out of the Suit and the Nice Shoes, and the Tie was driving him out of his mind. But he knew he couldn't do any of those things, so instead he talked to Ollie, giving a constant (but quiet) play-by-play of the goings-on in a sportscaster voice.

"About a million gazillion people are here," Billy told Ollie. "Lotta suits. Lotta grown-ups. Lotta fancy dresses. Lotta weird hair."

"Why do grown-ups do weird stuff to their hair?" asked Ollie.

"Beats me," said Billy. "The older the ladies get, the bigger the hair."

Later, after they sat down on long, hard benches and Billy had tucked the backpack at his feet because an old lady was squished up on one side of him and his mom was on the other, Billy (quietly) kept up the commentary:

"Nothing's happening, we're all just sitting here. . . . Wait . . .

wait. Now a bunch of guys in suits are standing up in front and they are waiting for something. . . . One guy has a *flower* on his suit! Now everybody's standing up again. . . . Is it over? No, not over. A line of ladies is coming down the middle. They're wearing really nice dresses. But one lady is wearing a really, *really* nice dress. Big. Puffy. White. That lady is smiling. . . . No, hold on a minute, she's crying. . . . No, she's smiling again. Okay, we're sitting down."

The sitting down went on for some time. Billy didn't have to say anything because a man in a long black coat was talking in a booming voice, and Billy knew Ollie could hear that, and then someone else was singing a song, and then someone else was reading a poem, and this seemed to go on forEVER, and Billy started to get superbored and kinda sleepy.

After a while the main lady in the big, puffy, white dress was talking, and then the man with the flower on his suit beside her

was talking. Then the lady in the dress was smiling and crying, and the man in the suit with her was holding her hand and he was smiling and looking like he was gonna cry. But then other people were smiling and crying too. When Billy looked around it seemed like lots of folks were smile-crying—including the old lady beside him and his own mom!

"Grown-ups crying like babies everywhere," Billy whispered to Ollie. "This is soooo weird."

But then suddenly the lady and man up front were kissing.

"Whoa, lots of slobber," Billy informed Ollie, ducking his head when it continued on and on. "Major slobber alert."

And then music started playing and everyone was standing up and cheering and clapping—and sorta shouting and talking, which Billy had thought was a huge no-no—and the next thing he knew he was being swept up into a whirl of people. Billy kept talking, kept relaying to Ollie all the strange things going on around him, never knowing that his words had stopped reaching Ollie, that his words were, in fact, falling on an empty backpack.

10
The truth about weddings (as told by the creeps)

The Creeps loved travel like snakes loved to slither. The trip to the Wedding while hiding under Billy's family car was just the kind of mission they relished. The reasons were simple:

1. It was really dangerous.

2. The underneath of a car is dark and smelly and scary.

3. They could sometimes steal pieces of the car's

insides that would make the car "break down" later, which was mean and a lot of trouble for the "Humes," as they called humans.

4. And all these things were bad, and bad to them was the purest kind of fun.

The Creeps had been spying on Billy and Ollie for days. They'd been listening at the windows or from flower beds. They'd made little tunnels into the walls of Billy's house and could travel from room to room without being seen. They'd spied from electrical outlets or tiny cracks along the floorboards.

So they knew everything about this Wedding. But they had planned on stealing Ollie while Billy went to the Wedding, when Ollie would be alone in the house. They'd found a way into Billy's room: an old mouse hole near his chest of drawers. That's where they were waiting when at the last second Billy had changed the

Parentals' minds. But the Creeps, in fact, weren't worried. They don't ever miss a beat.

Super Creep: Plan A is shot, boys. looks like a low ride. Go! Go! Go!

The Creeps could barely contain their excitement as they rushed through the walls and out from a loose floorboard under the front steps. From there it would be a quick but dangerous dash to the car in the driveway—for about ten feet they would be completely in the open, nothing to hide under, just an expanse of grass and concrete. But the Parentals were still locking the front door, so "GO, GO, GO!" the Super Creep ordered. The Creeps' little metal bits squeaked like giggles as they scurried out just an instant before Billy and his Parentals came down the stairs. The Creeps were already tucked behind the front tire by the time Billy walked by. Super Creep got a quick peek as Billy opened the car's back door.

Super Creep: All good. he's got the pack-'n-the-back. I can smell the Fave inside it!

As Billy's dad started the car, the Creeps scrambled into the wheel well and took their places on the axle. The car began to back up. In a few moments they were bouncing happily along, the road streaking beneath them. They squealed with pleasure at every sharp turn. Though they each had plenty of hooks and tiny magnets to hold them in place, there was still plenty of danger, and that made it even more fun. A sudden pothole almost jarred them all to their doom. They cheered in glee.

They were crazy with reckless courage and joy by the time the car stopped at the church. Once there, the job was fairly easy. The Humes were too distracted with being on time, or late, or missing the ceremony, or getting a good seat to pay much attention to them.

Still, Super Creep warned: If spotted, look trashy.

Despite there being dozens of people in the parking lot, the Creeps were almost seen only once. But they instantly collapsed on the ground like bits of trash, and no one even gave them a second glance.

Once they made their way inside the church, they moved quickly and stealthily. They snatched flowers from an arrangement on a table in the lobby and used them as camouflage until they crept under the pews. From there, the mission was a cinch. They could see Billy's pack-'n-the-back on the floor, four rows up. It was the only backpack. They crept quietly through the multitude of nice shiny shoes, pausing to leave a dark scuff on a lady's white high heels and scratching a really new-looking fancy shoe. The music and talking covered any noise they made. And by the time all the people were clapping at the ceremony's end, the Creeps had already left the church.

There wouldn't be another car ride for them on this mission.

It didn't matter. They knew every drainpipe in town. They were splashing through sewers and giggling over their successful mission at the very same time Billy was eating his first piece of wedding cake.

Billy had cake, but, in a small, dark sack, *they* had Ollie.

11

The hugest a-venture yet

For Billy, the rest of the Wedding was a bewildering blur. He had never seen so many grown-ups standing and talking *forever*. AND THEY TALKED SO LOUD. What is it with grown-ups and talking SO LOUD? They were always telling Billy to use his indoor voice, and here they all were, indoors, and practically shouting every. Single. WORD. THEY. SAID. And there were a bunch of guys playing musical instruments, which made everything ten times louder.

"That's a band," explained Billy's mother. "Aren't they fun?"

Billy didn't even try to explain to her his new understanding of grown-up fun: that it was strange and boring and loud and embarrassing. And he had been subjected to constant embarrassment for the past seven hundred hours. His parents had dragged Billy to about a million different grown-up people, and to each one of them his mom or dad would say in a really shouty way, "HELLLLLOOOOOO . . ." And then they would hug or shake hands and smile in a kinda alarming way and then they'd turn to Billy and say, "This is our little boy, Billy," and then . . . things . . . became . . . insane. Embarrassing. And insane. The grown-ups would scream, "He is so CUTE!" or "HE'S ADORABLE!" Sometimes they would add, "I COULD JUST EAT HIM UP!" *What? Are they CANNIBALS?* wondered Billy. And the grown-up men—every one!—would say, "Well, isn't he the handsome little man."

And almost every. Single. Time the grown-ups would put one of their hands on his head and do this weird mess-up-his-hair thing. Or worse. Hug him. And worse. KISS HIM ON THE CHEEK.

Billy could barely believe what was happening. *Weddings make grown-ups nuts,* he decided. He knew better than to try to tell Ollie now. It was too loud, and the grown-ups might see Ollie, and who knows how bad it would get after that. The hugging. The kissing. I mean, come *on*!

Finally, everyone sat down at a table. And his mom brought him a plate crowded with "fancy food," meaning horrible things wrapped up in other horrible things to disguise the horrible-ness, and Billy was no way, no how eating hidden asparagus! Blechhh! But then came the cake. The cake was actually impressive. It was huge and white and had a toy man and woman on top, which nobody played with. So Billy ate cake until he couldn't eat any more. And that's when he got sleepy.

The next thing he knew he was being slung over his dad's shoulder, being carried away from the Wedding.

"Where's Ollie?" he managed to mumble through a haze of sleepiness.

"Right here," his mom told him, holding up the backpack and giving it a pat.

Then Billy was in the backseat of the car, and he could see that the backpack was beside him, but then he must have fallen asleep again because next thing he knew, he was already in his pajamas, lying in his own bed.

"Where's Ollie?" Billy mumbled again as his mom pulled the covers up.

"Right here," she said again, gently placing the backpack near Billy's pillow.

Sleepily, Billy rolled over and reached inside, but when his fingers didn't touch the familiar plush softness, he bolted upright.

"Where's Ollie?" he nearly shouted, wide awake.

"Well, I'm sure he's . . . ," Billy's mom began, reaching a hand into the pack herself. When she realized it was empty she let out a little moan. "Oh honey, we told you not to take Ollie out at the wedding."

"I didn't!" Billy cried, checking the backpack once more. "I never took him out!"

"Maybe he fell out in the backseat," Dad suggested, and he hurried down to the car, but he came back shaking his head. "Not there, buddy. I'm sorry."

Billy stared at his parents. He felt like he was going to be sick. "We've got to find Ollie," he said. "We have to find him. Now."

It was late, and Billy's parents were tired. But they knew how important Ollie was to their son, and so they kept looking.

"Let's retrace our steps," Billy's dad suggested. "That always works for me when I've lost something."

Billy got out of bed and followed his parents out the front door. It was dark, of course, and it had gotten colder. Billy shivered as they checked the porch and then went down the steps and walked slowly along the sidewalk, stooping to look under the bushes.

"You're cold," Billy's mom said, and she tried to take him in her arms, but he shook her away and headed for the car.

His parents helped him search every nook and cranny of the car, but Ollie was nowhere to be found.

So they retraced their steps again, this time from the car to the porch and back up to Billy's bedroom.

"He must have fallen out at the wedding hall," Billy's mom said at last.

"Then we have to go back and get him! We have to retrace our steps to the Wedding." Billy started for the door again, but his mom stopped him. She knelt on the floor so they would be eye to eye.

"Listen, sweetie. It's too late to go back there tonight. The place will be closed by now. Everyone will have gone home already."

Billy shut his eyes. He imagined Ollie under the table, in the dark, in a strange place. Alone. Ollie had never slept alone.

And neither had Billy.

"We've got to go get Ollie," Billy said again firmly.

"I'm sorry, buddy." His dad put a hand on his shoulder and knelt down as well. "It's just too late tonight."

"It'll be okay, I promise," his mom said. She hugged him close. "We'll go get Ollie first thing in the morning. No one will take him. He'll be safe there, and we'll get him back and everything will be okay."

That's what they kept repeating: *everything will be okay*. And Billy wanted to believe them—he did. But he couldn't. He knew something was wrong; he knew Ollie was in trouble. He wasn't sure how he knew. But the feeling was there, and it wouldn't go away.

"Let's get you back in bed, sweetie," his mom said, and that's exactly what Billy did. He got back in bed, and he let himself be tucked in.

"Everything will be okay," his mom repeated one last time as she and his dad kissed him good night, and Billy nodded like he believed her, and closed his eyes.

Then he waited. He waited for his mom and dad to leave the room after watching him for a long while. He waited for their footsteps to fade down the hall, for the sound of their voices to fade as well. He waited until everything fell into silence and the only sounds were the creaks of the old house itself. He waited until the moon was at the very top corner of his window.

And then Billy opened his eyes.

He was going on his Hugest A-venture yet.

He was going to find Ollie.

12

ZoZo's Lair

Maybe this is a game. That's what Ollie thought at first. Some kind of wedding A-venture game where little flower dudes put you in a sack and took you somewhere and hid you. Kind of like hide-and-seek. Billy was good at hide-and-seek. He'd find Ollie in no time. Or was Ollie supposed to find Billy? And who were these little flower dudes, anyway?

But time passed—a lot of time, it felt like—and Ollie was still in the sack.

Wow, this is a really long game of hide-and-seek, Ollie thought. And an uncomfortable one. Ollie was bounced and dropped and knocked around. *The flower dudes play pretty rough.* And then just like that, he was dumped out of the sack and onto a cold, hard floor of a . . . What was this place?

The room wasn't like any room he had ever been in before. It was big—big enough to make echoes. And everything was shadowy.

Ollie was still hoping that this was hide-and-seek. "Ready or not, here I come!" His voice echoed sadly and then faded to silence.

"Okay. One, two, three, NOT it!" he tried. Again there was an echo, but this time there were also whispers: "Not it." "Nope. He's 'not it.'" "Not. Not. Not it."

As Ollie's eyes adjusted to the dark, he began to make out shapes hanging from the walls around him. Dozens of shapes. All whispering. He walked to one side of the room, and he saw that the shapes were toys. A whole lot of toys. Like him. But not like him. They were dirty and faded. Many were torn in places—lots of places—with stuffing sticking out of an arm or a leg, or an ear missing. Many were tied to the wall with jagged gnarls of wire. The wire looked to be wrapped very tightly—on some of the toys it had cut right into their fabric. Ollie thought this was a terrible way to store toys and started to forget about hide-and-seek and instead wonder who had done this, and why.

"Um, excuse me," Ollie said to a teddy bear who was closest and who seemed to be looking straight at him, although it was hard to tell exactly because one eye was gone and the other was held on by a sort of one-eyed glasses thing. "Are you one of Billy's parents' toys, like from the attic? Is this the attic? I'm not sure Billy will find me up here. I mean, he's never allowed to come up here by himself."

"Who's Billy?" the one-eye toy asked.

Ollie looked at him in surprise. Maybe One-Eye Teddy had been in the attic a long, long time, and no one had ever told him about Billy.

"Billy is my boy. He lives in this house. This is the attic, right?"

"No boys live here," said another nearby toy, a kind of elephant.

"And this is not the attic," said a stubby-armed dino.

One-Eye Teddy said, "You're at Zozo's."

"What's a Zozo?" Ollie asked, thinking that maybe it was the name of Billy's dad's favorite toy.

"You'll see," One-Eye Teddy said, turning his one eye away.

Again, there was silence, and Ollie tried to get his bearings. Perhaps, he thought, this whole thing was related to the Wedding somehow.

A poor moldy bunny with a tiny carrot stitched onto one paw interrupted his thoughts. "You're a favorite, aren't you?"

Ollie nodded. "Billy's favorite."

"I was a favorite," Elephant spoke up. "Once. We were all favorites . . . once," he added with a sigh.

"Who made you a favorite?" Ollie asked Elephant.

The elephant's plastic eyes brightened for a moment and then just as quickly dimmed to a dull black. "It was a little girl. . . ." He trailed off.

"He can't remember her name," Carrot Bunny explained. "That's what happens when you've been at Zozo's long enough. You forget your kid." The other toys muttered in agreement.

"That's impossible. I'll never forget my kid," Ollie exclaimed. "I'll never forget Billy!"

Silence again. Dead silence. Ollie could feel the toys watching him. Not just Dino and Elephant, but all the others too—those unidentifiable shapes in the darkness.

When One-Eye Teddy spoke again, he didn't sound

mean—only as if he were stating a simple fact. "Just wait, you'll see."

But Ollie didn't want to wait. He didn't like this place at all. It was dark and it smelled bad, kind of like the cellar in Billy's house—damp and musty—only much, much worse.

"I'm ready to leave now."

Ollie didn't mean to say it out loud, but he must have because a murmuring went through the shapes in response.

"Sometimes a toy escapes," Elephant conceded.

"But the Creeps always bring them back," Carrot Bunny added.

"Are those the guys who brought me here?" asked Ollie.

"Yep," said One-Eye Teddy. "And they keep ya here."

"Well, they're not keeping me. I'm leaving," Ollie said. "And I'll bring my Billy to help you get away, too." Then he started to look for a way out.

The toys continued to watch him with their dull eyes.

"The newbies never believe," Ollie heard one of them say.

And Ollie, who had felt fairly brave until that moment, suddenly felt a flicker of unbrave. He began to tremble, just enough to make the small bell-heart in his center begin to jingle. If the other toys heard the sound, they did not comment. But Ollie heard it, felt it, and it made him think of Billy and Billy's mom and how she had, with her own two hands, made Ollie so he could look after Billy. And that helped him feel stronger.

I will get out of here, he told himself. Billy looked left, then patchpaw, then left again, and saw there was a doorway that was dark and damp, so he figured that that must be the way out. Ollie trembled again—his bell-heart giving a jingle—this time, though, from excitement as he made his way through the shadows. Then a voice rang out.

"IT'S NOT THE ONE!" It was unlike any voice Ollie had ever heard.

And there it was again. "IT'S NOT MY FAVORITE!"

The voice was pure anger; it was hate—things that Ollie had never really known but now sensed. Ollie turned around and saw what must have been, at one time, a toy. A clown toy.

Ollie knew about clowns. He had been to the circus with Billy. He knew they were supposed to be happy, funny creatures. But often they were not. Even when their lips were smiling, their eyes often gave away their sadness.

This clown standing before Ollie, however, did not even attempt to smile. His red mouth was turned down in a terrible sneer, and his black eyebrows formed a deep V across his wide forehead. The paint on his face was chipped and flaking, and rust seemed to be eating him away. His pointed hat was bent at a sharp angle. But his eyes were not sad. His eyes were most frightening. They were black as coal, and they seemed to look inside of Ollie.

"He's just a plush," Zozo growled to his Creeps, who walked with him. "He's not it."

"But he's a favorite, Zozo," the Super Creep stated. Zozo turned his glare toward the him.

"I mean 'boss'!" the Super Creep amended, groveling.

Zozo made a sound of disgust. "He's a Homemade, too."

Ollie had never really known fear. But what he was feeling right now, this terrible uncertainty— Who was this? Why am I here? What do they want? The not knowing—these things must be fear. But Billy's parents always said, "Don't be afraid," and so did Billy, so at that moment Ollie decided he wouldn't be afraid.

"I'm Ollie," Ollie said, his voice not sounding a bit frightened. He cleared his throat and made himself speak louder. "That's my name. Ollie. And your name is Zozo. So it's kind of like 'Ollie.' You have two Zs and I've got two Ls, and Zs are the last letter of the alphabet, and you've got two Os, but I've only got one. I wish I had two Zs and two Os in my name. You have a cool name."

There was dead silence. No one spoke. No one moved.

Then there was a strange sound. A kind of rusty, garbled sound.

Laughter, Ollie realized. Zozo was laughing.

"Funny!" Zozo said. He looked at his Creeps. "That's funny, isn't it?"

The Creeps got the hint—fast. They started laughing. Louder and louder because it seemed to please their boss.

"Yeah, that's real funny!" Creep 1 said.

"A gas!" Creep 2 added.

"'Zozo,' is a 'cool' name," Zozo said. And then his laughter stopped abruptly. It took a moment longer for the Creeps to realize the joke was done, and the Super Creep had to bang Creeps 1 and

2 on the head so they would stop laughing, but finally there was silence again.

"You and I are *nothing* alike, little plush," Zozo sneered. Then he turned to the Creeps. "Tie him up!"

Before Ollie could utter a protest, the Creeps grabbed him and took him high up along the curved ceiling of the room. There, among the other sad favorites, they began to twine him tightly to an old, jagged hook that stuck out from the damp concrete. As they yanked the wire ever tighter, Ollie feared his seams would rip right open. The tiny tin bell of his heart made a sharp jangle.

"Wait!" Zozo bellowed from below. Now the Creeps froze. Ollie wasn't sure whether to be hopeful or scared. Zozo stared up at him. "What was that?"

The Creeps weren't sure what Zozo was asking about. Creep 2 moved one of his arms back and forth. It made a metallic sound similar to Ollie's bell. "That sound, Boss?" he asked.

Zozo continued to stare, his eyes boring into them all. The rest of the Creeps hurried to demonstrate their different squeaky, jangly elbows, ankles, arms, legs, and heads until they made a rather displeasing little symphony of metal.

At last Zozo spat out, "ENOUGH!" He turned away in disgust and walked away from them.

"Ollie," the Creeps started taunting, "with two *L*s!"

"Um, how long will I be here?" Ollie managed to ask. "I mean, Billy will be expecting me by tuck-in time."

One of the Creeps started laughing. "The Bunny-Teddy Plushy wants to go home."

"He wants to know how long he'll be here."

More laughter started up. "Yeah, that's a good one."

Ollie tried to laugh too. But before he could, the first Creep shouted, "FOREVER!"

Ollie stopped laughing. But the Creeps did not. Their laughs echoed long after they clambered away to some other part of the nasty network of tunnels.

Ollie closed his eyes and tried to believe he was back home, in Billy's bed. He tried to imagine what Billy was doing at that moment. He tried to understand how to make forever not be in this place.

13
string cheese and light sabers

The entire time Billy had waited for his parents to leave, for their voices to fade and the house to fall silent, he'd been doing more than struggling to stay awake. He'd been planning. He had been planning his OLLIE DANGER RESCUE NIGHTTIME SECRET MISSION OF SECRECY for what had seemed like at least 217 hours, or maybe all the way past midnight. He looked at his cuckoo clock with the little blue bird that came out every hour, but Billy never really knew what time it was because he'd knocked off both the hands when he was "little," which was actually only five months earlier, but that seemed so long ago that he had to have been little.

He used a lot of consideration as he readied his backpack for this mission. "Consideration" was one of the longest words he knew. Con Sid Eration. Why was "consideration" so long when it really just meant "think"? Maybe it was just another grown-up way to make something more complicated than it really was. Grown-ups did that all the time.

But all this consideration and thinking it over had kept Billy's mind busy and very unsleepy. His backpack was filled with basically everything he thought he might need:

1. **His flashlight saber**. It had a broken speaker so it didn't make sword-like noises anymore, which was okay because Billy was trying to be supersecret

and that meant being superquiet. The flashlight part of the saber was important. It helped him see (sort of, anyway) in the dark, and since it was past midnight, there was gonna be loads of dark. And dark was, well . . . scary, no matter what anybody said. Dark when you're a littlish kid is scary, and since Billy was by himself, dark was gonna be a really big, fill-all-the-air-around-him-and-then-some SCARY THING. *Plus*, the flashlight saber was a major protection device in case of dogs, or werewolves, or crazy zombies or monsters of ANY KIND.

2. **Crayons.** Billy wasn't sure why he needed crayons. They just made him feel safe.

3. **String cheese and goldfish crackers.** In case the journey was for a long time and he would starve.

4. **Four green-apple lollipops.** They tasted good, and Billy sometimes pretended that they made him invisible.

5. **A couple handfuls of plastic action figures and one tiny, soft, plastic Pegasus.** You just never knew when you'd need some toy action figures. Maybe they'd come magically alive and save Billy. Right? And a tiny, soft, plastic Pegasus was something everyone should have with them all the time no matter what.

That was pretty much it. Everything else was in his hoodie pockets. His parents' cell phone numbers. His address. Some more string cheese.

Billy changed into his favorite pajamas. Put on his fastest shoes (they had some kinda air cushions in them). He squooshed his pillows in a lump under the covers, so it would seem like he was sleeping in his bed, and then he turned for one last look at his room before he tiptoed down the hall.

"So long, guys," he said to everything. "I'll be back as soon as I can."

14

The Room of DARK DEEDS

As he settled in his workroom, Zozo was troubled. This room was perhaps his only comfort. This was the room where Zozo tried to change his past and seek his revenge. It was in this room where he made the first of his Creeps, taking frayed bits of left-over toys from the old carnival—the toys who had never known the company of a child. They had never sat in the grass under a tree and been a hero in a pretend adventure. They had never been clutched tightly while racing down a slide. They had never been hugged under the covers during a terrible thunderstorm. They had never been the gentle buffer against sadness, or felt the joys of being tossed and hugged and played with. They had never been the one thing that made everything all right for a kid.

So, these sagging, never-loved toys were perfect for Zozo's needs. They'd only ever been with Zozo, and so they had nothing other than his darkened ways to learn from. But Zozo took advantage of this by making them do things he could not. Zozo had become rusted and slow. And truth be told, he feared the outside world. He could not control what happened there. But in this place, this room of dark deeds, he ruled absolutely, and the Creeps did anything he ordered. Rough and quick and mean were the Creeps. They could sneak about with such stealth and ease that even birds, squirrels, and dogs seldom heard them coming. Favorite toys didn't have a chance once the Creeps set their sights on them.

They were, as a whole, a sneaky but jolly lot. They enjoyed being Creeps. They liked being bad and stealing toys. But when Zozo was quiet and still, as he was this evening, they grew even quieter and more still. Zozo was fearsome when he had "the quiets," as they called these moods. It meant that Zozo was "remembering," and that was a thing that never ended well.

Zozo sat at his large worktable, which was littered with well-organized bits and pieces of old toys: arms, legs, heads, bodies, ears, tails, fabric, thread, and metal shards, as well as rusty springs, staples, and screws and nuts with bolts—things similar to what he'd used to make Creeps. But in the middle of the table, on a white piece of nice, clean fabric, there lay a toy who was obviously special, for it was constructed with extreme care and exacting craft. It was a dancer, and it was obviously meant to be Nina. But despite all the detailed care, it somehow was not Nina. The fabric and colors and face were very close, having been pieced together from snippets of favorites that matched as closely as Zozo could manage to the Nina he remembered. But very close can still be a long, long way from what you want, or need, or hope for.

As Zozo now sat in his old rotting throne, its gold paint nearly peeled away, staring silently at this lifeless doll of his memories and his making, he said nothing. The Creeps were worried. And they were wise for being worried. For Zozo was remembering a sound, a sound he'd heard long, long ago. A jingling.

15
Midnight in the Hallway of giant monkeys

Billy walked down the hall that led to his front door. It was dark except for a flickering glow coming from the den. *The TV is on*, Billy noticed, but he wasn't worried. It was late enough. His parents always fell asleep. Especially if the show was good. Still, he peered carefully into the den. Yep. There they were, his mom and dad splayed on the L-shaped couch like ragdolls, sound asleep.

They'd been watching that channel, the one with all the black-and-white movies, from a time his dad called "back in the day." Billy found these movies very interesting but strange. There were no colors in back-in-the-day movies. Just white and gray and black. And the dads all wore hats, and the moms wore tight dresses, and the cars were big and roundish. *And* ALL the people had smoke coming out of their mouths as they talked. And they talked with these weird little sticks called cigarettes between their lips that had smoke coming out of them too. And people talked really fast. Plus, everybody seemed to have guns. They'd stand around and talk fast, with smoke pouring out of their mouths, and almost always after a while they'd all pull out guns, even the moms, and then the music would get really loud and everybody—moms, dads, grandparent people—would start shooting.

Billy had given a lot of thought to all this and had decided that people really had anger issues in the black-'n'-white times.

But tonight the black-and-white channel was showing something even stranger than usual. Billy could hardly believe what he was seeing, and he felt himself drawn to the screen. Without realizing it he had walked into the room and stood gaping: a gorilla—a really, really big gorilla, a big-as-a-house-gorilla—was standing at the top of a tall, pointy building. Not only that, but he was holding a regular-sized lady, and she looked like a toy in the giant gorilla's hand.

And there were airplanes; funny-looking airplanes with two sets of wings, and the guys flying the planes weren't even all the way inside of them—their heads were sticking out, like, in the air! And they were shooting at the giant gorilla with these log-sized guns tied to the front of the plane, and the gorilla was really mad, which made a lotta sense to Billy, and the gorilla put the girl down, and she was screaming, which also made sense to Billy, 'cause she didn't have on a coat or anything and it had to be cold way up there, and then the gorilla grabbed one of the planes and flung it down and it crashed into a building.

Then some guy said, "We gotta rescue Ann!" and Billy thought, *Oh, the gorilla's girl's name is Ann, and they are trying to save her from the gorilla. . . .*

Saving . . .

Saving . . . Oh! Billy blinked. That's what *he* was supposed to be doing. He was supposed to be saving Ollie. He tiptoed quietly back out of the room, past his still-sleeping parents. He couldn't understand how they could fall asleep watching stuff this awesome, and he took one more glance at the TV. The gorilla was still raging. And as Billy inched down the hall, he could hear the big guy's mighty roars. As he opened the front door as quietly as possible, he could hear the planes and the clatter of their guns that sounded sharp and fast, like a stick brushed across a fence.

And as he shut the door and left the house, Billy faced the great dark of the night. He knew what he was about to do was highly illegal, and big-time in trouble (if he got caught), and was maybe even gonna be scarier than all get out, but in that moment his mind had gone to someplace new. It was a place where pretend and real were all mixed up and he couldn't quit thinking about that gorilla, because the gorilla looked like he was in trouble and Billy felt sorry for him. Maybe the gorilla had to get in trouble for a good reason. And he thought, *I hope that was a real story. I hope that wasn't pretend.* And he wished the big gorilla well, and hoped he'd be all right.

16
The DARK CARNIVAL

Imprisoned toys are a sad and hopeless lot. But whenever a new favorite is brought in, they rouse, just a little. The newbies always gave them a glimmer their former lives. Now, with the arrival of this new favorite, Ollie, they started asking him about "his boy."

"Is he nice, your boy?" asked Carrot Bunny.

"Oh, yeah!" Ollie said enthusiastically. "He is major nice. Nice. Nicer. Nicest!"

"What size is he?" asked an octopus who was missing at least one leg.

"Well, he started out a little bigger than me, but that was six birthdays ago. Now he's six birthdays and a half big."

All the toys said things like "aaaaaah" or "uh-huh" or "hmmm," as if they understood. As if they remembered. So Ollie told them all about Billy. How he had been very leaky when he was little, and how they were always together, and what color Billy's hair was—sorta like dirt mixed with sand—and how Billy smelled after a bath, and about tuck-ins, and slobber kisses, and he told them about huge A-ventures and yum, and the more he talked, the more the other toys liked it, and Ollie realized that he liked it too. Talking about Billy made him feel safe and happy and less unheroic, even though he was tied up here in this strange toy prison.

And that feeling was somehow reaching out and helping all

the poor sad toys *feel* and *remember*. Then Ollie began to explain how Billy had a hole in his heart, but how it was gone now. The doctor had said so. Then Ollie proudly told them that he had a heart too; it was a bell, sewn into his chest by Billy's mom. He thumped his chest with one free hand, and the bell tinkled just loud enough for everyone to hear. Everyone, including Zozo.

"Where did the bell come from?" asked One-Eye Teddy.

Ollie was about to answer when they heard a terrible smashing sound from Zozo's chamber. It was followed by an explosion of shouting so loud, the toys quaked, dust and grit falling from them and adding a dirty haze to the already dark chamber.

"BRING ME THAT HOMEMADE!" Zozo was bellowing.

Ollie could hear the clamor of the Creeps bumping into one another and bumbling around, and he knew that they were coming for him. At the same time, he felt something tugging on his foot. He looked down and his eyes went wide. A tower of other favorites, balancing one on top of the other, like in a circus, were reaching up to him.

"Is this a plan?" Ollie asked One-Eye, who, at the top of the tower, was pulling his foot.

"Yep!" One-Eye said. "It's our plan for your escape!"

"Well, okay, then."

Then One-Eye yanked Ollie's leg really hard and pulled him free. The force of the yank, however, sent the whole stack of them tumbling to the floor. Zozo was still yelling, and the Creeps sounded just steps away.

"Hurry!" Carrot Bunny urged Ollie. "We'll hold them off!"

Elephant pointed to a dark place in the wall. "That's the tunnel. It'll take you out of here."

Ollie didn't need to be told twice. He rushed toward the opening. It took him a moment to realize he was the only one running. He swung back around.

"It's too late for us! We've forgotten too much. You still remember!" Elephant insisted. Ollie looked from Elephant to the others. They were all nodding. The Creeps were swarming into the prison room.

Toy after toy broke their bonds. They jumped and slugged and threw themselves at the Creeps.

"Go!" Elephant yelled.

"I'll come back, I promise," Ollie told them, meaning it with all his heart. Then he turned and ran.

The tunnel was twisted and dark. Ollie could hear the Creeps screaming for him in the midst of the sounds of struggle and fighting. The Creeps were on to him! They knew he had escaped, and they were chasing him! The echoing was like a nightmare. Sometimes it seemed like the Creeps were right behind him, and sometimes it seemed like they had somehow surged ahead.

Ollie kept running. He ran until he didn't think he could run anymore. Then the tunnel ended abruptly, without warning, and he was pitched forward, into the darkness, until he landed— *thud*—in a patch of soft, oozy sludge and water. Ollie swam toward what little light he could see up ahead until he came to a muddy bank of grassy land. He didn't like water. It reminded him of being in the washing machine. And this time, he felt even more alone.

Ollie struggled to stand in the mud. He looked up and saw the starry night sky. He was aboveground again! That was good. Then he heard the distant rumble of thunder. Not so good. The stars began to dim as black clouds swept across the sky. He had to keep moving.

He turned to look behind him from where he'd been, and saw a giant smiling head staring down at him, with a sign that said TUNNEL OF LOVE. And drifting in the shallow water at the mouth of the tunnel was an old, sad-looking swan boat. He was in the Dark Carnival Place. He was sure of it! The place where kids were never supposed to go.

Now all he had to do was face the huge, dark night and some-how find home and Billy.

17
fireflies

It is one thing to make the decision to go on the Hugest A-venture Ever in order to find your favorite toy. It is quite another to actually do it.

Billy had gotten as far as the front porch. He stood staring out at the dark. He knew he must walk down the steps and then walk down the sidewalk—that part would be easy. He'd done *that* a million times. But he wasn't quite sure what to do afterward.

Had they turned right or left when his dad had driven to the

Wedding? Billy closed his eyes. First, he had to make sure he remembered which was left and which was right. *Okay. I draw with my . . . right hand,* he reminded himself. He held his right hand up at the elbow, which made him look like he was sort of waving.

Ollie didn't agree with the terms "right" and "left." He always said "patchpaw" and "the other way." His right hand (or paw) had a small patch on its underside. He and Billy had gotten caught in a sticker bush one day, and they both came out a bit worse for it. Ollie had ripped the stitching on his right paw, so Billy's mom added a yellow patch to close it up. Bill had needed Band-Aids on his chin, his elbow, and coincidentally, the palm of his right hand. Ollie was fascinated by the Band-Aids, which he called "patches," and he had taken great pleasure in the fact that he and Billy had matching "patchpaws," even though Billy's had a dinosaur on it and Ollie's matched the color of his paw.

So, Billy stood there with his right hand in the air, and he found himself feeling kind of brave, because thinking of rescuing Ollie made him that way. He also realized that his dad's car had gone right when they backed out of the driveway. *Patchpaw it is,* Billy decided, and turned left. *Oh wait,* thought Billy. *That's the other way.* So he turned patchpaw. Why was keeping that straight so hard? Anyway. The park was on the right, and he could walk all the way to the park, no problem. He'd been doing that on his own for a whole year now. No big deal.

Except . . . he had never walked to the park in the dark before. Who knew that the dark could be . . . well . . . so **dark?**

Things got better when he reached a street lamp. The street lamp created a whole big circle of light, and it was the perfect place to rest between the darkness. That's exactly how Billy thought of it: resting inside a nice, round, warm circle of light before plunging into the dark again.

Billy did a quick count. There were eight more street lamps till the park. And then there was a big light at the entrance. Billy rested for a while. No one else was out. The whole neighborhood seemed totally empty. It was so strange and quiet and alone feeling. He knew that people were inside all of the houses. But it didn't *feel* like they were. Then a slight breeze sent leaves tumbling and tapping down the sidewalks like zillions of tiny skeletons sneaking all around him. Billy decided he should stop resting and start walking, and fast. He *wasn't* scared, NOT AT ALL, but he did feel really relieved each time he reached a streetlight. He felt relief until he reached the park. Because then he remembered: the park was *across the street.*

Which meant Billy would have to cross a street. Alone. Without Mr. B. Without a grown-up.

Billy heaved a huge, long, worried "this is impossible" sigh. He had come so far *on his own!* But he couldn't cross a street alone. It was against the law. For a moment he wondered if an alarm would go off or something, and the cops would swoop down and scoop him up and put him in jail, and then he'd never find Ollie. But he realized that he had never ever heard any alarm go off when any other kid had crossed the street alone. So . . .

He took a deep breath.

He looked right (or patchpaw) and then left, and then patchpaw again as he had been taught. He did it three more times. No cars, no people—just spooky leaves sounding all Halloweeny. Then he put one foot onto the street, and then the other.

And *nothing* happened!

Wow.

Billy hustled across the street, just in case the alarm was slow or something. And boy, did it take a long time to get across. It was just a regular street, but being by himself made it seem twenty times wider than usual. It seemed to take *forever* to get across. But finally he was on the other side. He waited. No alarms. No police. All clear. Just the wind and the leaves.

And the spookiness.

Wow. Wait till Ollie hears about this, Billy thought, but his moment of victory quickly vanished. He had no idea which way to go next. This was a big problem. Who was he kidding, anyway? He was just a kid. How could he ever make it all the way to the Wedding place on his own in the dark, and rescue Ollie?

He pulled out his light saber. Because from here on, there was a lot of dark.

And . . . and . . . what if he never found Ollie—not on this night, or any other? What if he never got the chance to tell him about this huge A-venture? But he remembered a movie he'd seen on his parents' movie channel. It was in bright, bright color. And it was scary but wonderful. There was a girl with red shoes who wanted to go home, and all she had to do was find a man named Oz. To find this magic Oz man, these little bitty people who sang a lot told the girl to follow a yellow brick road. Billy wished the roads around him were some kind of color, as THAT WOULD BE HELPFUL, but they were all dark gray.

Billy stood there at the edge of the park, starting to feel scared. How many streetlights were there till he got to the Wedding place? He didn't remember his dad's car making many turns. He looked past the park's entrance to the next row of streetlights, and that's when he noticed a glow, a strange glow, just ahead of him. It was different from the glow of a street lamp—more like a cloud. A cloud made up of lots of tiny sparkling lights.

Fireflies! That's what they were. Hundreds of them. Hovering just above Billy's head.

The sight was so . . . ghostly but beautiful, and strangely unscary. Plus, he loved fireflies. Why, he and Ollie used to catch them in jars. . . . But wait! Something peculiar was happening. The fireflies were starting to move as one. The cloud of fireflies began to drift through the gate of the park. And Billy knew he was meant to follow them. They would be his yellow brick road.

18
A GAME of CATCH

Ollie had been running from Zozo for a pretty long time. He'd run through the Dark Carnival without even noticing what a bizarre place it was. He did not think of going right or left or "patchpaw" or "the other way." He just ran as fast as was possible for a toy who was a little over a foot high, with legs less than six inches long. He knew he was being chased by the Creeps, and he knew they were sneaky, fast, and probably very good at following and catching toys who made "a break for it." So, he just went blind crazy fast as he could. He tore through mud and ditches and weeds and sticker bushes so quickly that even when a piece of him snagged on a twig or a thorn, he ripped himself loose and kept going.

And as time passed and he still wasn't caught, he slowed but only slightly, just enough so that he could think more clearly. *I should try not to leave tracks they can follow,* he told himself. *I should not let my scarf unravel on a sticker bush. They will find the thread and know where I've been.* And these thoughts calmed him, and he began to run and jump and dodge with a confidence he had never felt before. He was like Super Ollie, his scarf flapping behind him like a cape. He began to hold his arms out in front of him, like all superheroes do when they fly, and for a moment he actually wondered if he could, in fact, fly.

He had flown many times when pretending with Billy, and pretending felt real, but he knew it was different. Pretending was something he and Billy did together. Pretending was like a strange and wonderful place where things happened the way they wished them to. It was Real Life Plus with spaceships and dinosaurs and monsters and powers so super that you could always get out of trouble and save the day. Ollie liked pretending almost more than anything. So, on this crazy night of real life, he pretended that he could fly. Fly over the ground and trees and straight to Billy. And for a few moments he felt the great power of his own hopes as he believed that he was flying, and in his pretend he flew into the window of Billy's room and landed on the pillow where he always slept with his boy Billy.

But suddenly, he was jerked into the air. For a moment, just a moment, Ollie thought he had pretended *so hard* that he had broken through to real life! But then he realized the truth: he had been plucked up into the mouth of a large black dog, and the dog was running very fast. So fast that to Ollie, it did feel like flying.

Ollie must have been so lost in pretending that he hadn't heard the dog coming, but now he heard the dog's coarse huffing as they galloped from the trees and toward a street lined with parked cars.

Ollie's experience with dogs was very limited. Billy's family didn't have one, but Ollie had watched dogs in the park with their people. Dogs seemed to belong to people the way toys belonged to kids. He saw that people talked to dogs, and though dogs didn't exactly talk back, they did seem to understand. Sort of. Dogs didn't always do what their people told them to do, which Ollie found odd. Dogs would just run off, and then their person would yell things, like "Come back, Rex! I mean it right now you bad dog come here I said COME HERE."

Ollie didn't think the dogs were actually "bad." It seemed to him they were just distracted by the general funness of the world. The same way Billy would sometimes get, and then he and Billy would break a few laws when no grown-ups were watching. So,

Ollie assumed that this dog was doing the same thing, but then he remembered that pretending was sometimes quite loud, especially when flying, and that perhaps he had been making super flying sounds, so maybe, *just maybe*, the dog heard Ollie's pretending and was trying to help him.

"Ummm. Hi, Mr. Dog Person," Ollie began. "Thank you for giving me a ride. I guess you would know where Billy is?"

The dog didn't answer; he just continued to run and was now on the street. Though he did glance down at Ollie, as if surprised the toy was talking.

Ollie was, of course, worried about being in the street, especially since the dog hadn't looked both ways.

"Say there, Mr. Dog Friend, you know, it's against the law to be in the street without looking—"

But before Ollie could finish, he was yanked out of the dog's mouth and thrown into the air, and Ollie wasn't sure if he was

flying or falling. And before he could even figure *that* out, he felt himself being caught. He was in the hand of a boy, a bigger-than-Billy boy, who was riding on a skateboard. IN THE STREET. AT NIGHT. All Ollie could think was, *This kid is some other kind of kid. He does a lot of "against the law." He's kind of a Danger Kid.*

Then Ollie noticed there were several of these Danger Kids riding skateboards in the street, and the dog was running along with them. He wondered if they were a pack. Like wolves.

"Speedy brought us a toy!" yelled the kid who held Ollie.

"Lemme see!" said one of the other kids, and suddenly, Ollie was tossed through the air and caught by the Lemme See Kid.

"What's he supposed to be?" Lemme See said with a laugh.

"Gimme a look," said another kid. And just like that Ollie was tossed and caught again.

"Looks like a teddy rabbit!" shouted Gimme a Look. And then

Ollie was tossed, and not very nicely, from one laughing Danger Kid to another, as if he were a ball in a very unfun game of catch.

"Look out, here it comes!"

"Heads up!"

"Whoever drops him has to go home!"

The boys wove quickly up to the sidewalk, back down to the asphalt, and then around the parked cars, and Ollie was very ready to be dropped. And sure enough, Lemme See threw him so far that nobody caught him. He landed in the grass near a curb, and none of the Danger Kids came back to find him. They just laughed as they skated away. Speedy the Dog, however, did come sniffing after him. Ollie felt his wet nose on his back, his hot breath all over him as the dog flipped Ollie over, about to snatch him up again.

"Come on, Speedy, leave it!" yelled Gimme a Look.

Instantly, the dog lifted his head, turned, and disappeared into the night.

Ollie sat there, stunned. Those were older kids. The kind of kids Billy told him about. The ones who forgot their toys. Would Billy ever become one of those kids? And somewhere deep inside him came a feeling he could not understand. His hope came up against what he had just seen and experienced, and he wondered about the difference between pretending and real life. He did not like feeling that one might be stronger than the other.

19

when pretending gets nutty

Billy followed the small cloud of fireflies as they slowly drifted
and curled through the deep night shadows of the park. Darkness
transformed the park in ways that were surprising. The swings,
which were usually full and busy, now swayed at a sluggish and
ghostly pace in the steady evening wind. The long, low limbs of
the oak trees, which during the day were so enticing to climb,
lurched to and fro like giant fingers stiffly reaching for anything
that came close. Places where Billy had played with Ollie and his

pals seemed no longer welcoming and friendly, but rather mysterious, gloomy, and even a little frightening.

Billy tried to pretend that Hannah of the Runny Nose was with him, and Perry of the Sticks and even Muddy Butch, but in his pretending, they appeared as ghost versions of themselves, all pale and dim with eyes gleaming and eerie smiles.

"Yikes!" he whispered, quickly closing his eyes and shaking his head to make the pretend go away. He'd forgotten that sometimes pretending did what it wanted, especially when he was scared. It was like pretending decided to play a trick on him and made him see things he really did not want to see. Especially at night. In the dark.

Closets, the dark under beds, and shadowy places made pretending a "tricky customer." Usually, Billy sort of liked that about pretending. It made it more like real life 'cause real life almost never did what you wanted. But Billy only liked it if Ollie was with him when the pretending got nutty. Being afraid with somebody, especially Ollie, made afraidness a lot less fearsome.

But the fireflies helped Billy feel better. And so he kept following them. They were real-life things that seemed made up and magic. Like rainbows and glowworms and hummingbirds and magnets. Fireflies were so cool that you almost couldn't believe they were real, and they made Billy wonder what else there was in the world that seemed too good to be true.

So he kept following them deeper into the park, much farther than Billy had ever gone before, to a part of the park that seemed wild and overgrown. From this point on, Billy wasn't sure if he knew the way home. So he decided to leave a trail he could follow. A trail of action figures from his backpack. The first one he pulled out was one of his oldest, Grongo the Twig Man of Planet Zoxxo. Billy had had Grongo for so long he couldn't remember *not* having him. He placed the little action figure on top of a fair-sized rock that was at the place where Billy decided the park ended and the unknown rest of the world began. "Stay steady, Grongo," he said. "I'm counting on you."

As Billy walked away, he was sure that he was being followed by monsters. But he held his light saber tight and wouldn't look back. And then the battery in the light saber died. Then the wind began to blow even harder, and the fireflies were being pushed all around, breaking up and spreading out in a way that made it difficult for Billy to know which way to go or which ones to follow. Then it started to thunder. Just a rumble or two at first, but soon louder and closer. This was "bad news" and "bummer" and "in trouble" all put together.

By the time the rain started and the first flash of lightning lit the sky, Billy felt like he had lost just about all his brave. Some fireflies scattered under the trees. But most of them had taken shelter under a strange-looking structure. It was a huge smiling boy with a pointy hat! And for a few seconds, Billy was sure his make-believe had gone completely nutty. A GIANT SITTING BOY?! Then he remembered—this boy was made of wood and plaster. This boy was the entrance to the old carnival. The place the other kids called the Dark Carnival. The giant boy looked pretty creepy, but the rain fell harder and the lightning and thunder were close. So Billy huddled under the boy as the storm raged all around. He felt so lost. As lost as a little boy could feel. But he was not alone. The fireflies rested there with him. Several crawled around onto his hand as he shivered, lighting up for just an instant and then going dim and lighting up again. But it was hard not to see monsters and ghosts and skeletons. So Billy thought only of home and his parents and his best friend, Ollie.

20

CAN MAN

Ollie had not been sitting by the curb very long when the storm began to blow near. He had never been outside during a storm, and so he found the wind and thunder very interesting.

I wish Billy were here, he thought for the umpteenth time that night. *Storms aren't that scary. They're kind of*—he searched for a word that felt right—*bigtastic!* A couple of fat raindrops smacked Ollie on the head. *Except for the getting wet part.* He hoped he wouldn't get any wetter. Being too wet was a major bummer. Ollie could barely walk when he got too wet. But as he wondered about his wet level, he heard a squeaking sound; it was coming closer and closer.

The Creeps! he instantly worried, swinging around in the direction of the squeaking. Through the rain, he could just make out a man slowly pushing a shopping cart. Odd, but at least it wasn't the Creeps. The man was wearing several black garbage bags as a sort of raincoat, singing quietly under his breath. Ollie recognized the song and the man. Can Man! Ollie and Billy saw him in the neighborhood every week or so.

Sure enough, the man leaned over and picked up an empty soda can from the side of the road. He then stood it up straight and stomped on it once. The can went perfectly flat. He tossed it in one of the many bulging garbage bags in his cart. Ollie figured they were all filled with stomped cans.

Can Man looked up, scanning the pavement and curb

ahead of him for more cans. His eyes fell upon Ollie.

Uh-oh.

Ollie hoped the man wouldn't think *he* was a can.

Can Man pushed his cart right up to him and stared at the toy for longer than Ollie thought was okay. *He's gonna stomp me for sure.*

Then the Can Man said, "You need some cover, little man. It's raining too hard for the likes of you." The man began to pull on one of his trash bags till he peeled off a piece that was the size of a Kleenex. Picking Ollie up, Can Man tenderly wrapped the piece of trash bag over Ollie's head and shoulders like a tiny poncho.

"Somebody lost you, little man," said Can Man with gentle concern. "And they will come lookin' for you, and they probably don't want you all squishy."

Ollie was relieved—it didn't seem like Can Man thought *he* was a can. He studied Can Man's face while he finished making the poncho. It was an older face. Older than Billy's parents', for

sure. But Ollie liked it. The deep creases and wrinkles around the eyes and mouth had a sad but friendly look. Kind of like an old toy.

Can Man gave Ollie's poncho a final satisfied tug. He stared at Ollie for the longest time, the creases on his face deepening. Rain trickled down onto Ollie. The expression on Can Man's face was bewildering. It wasn't sad, really, or angry, but something Ollie had never seen before. It was like many feelings mixed together. Time seemed to stand completely still. Only the rain fell. Can Man's face was like a statue's now, but his eyes were very alive. It was like he was seeing past Ollie. Into another time. Ollie suddenly thought, *Maybe he's remembering. Maybe he had a toy like me.* Can Man finally stirred and wiped the dripping water from Ollie's eyes and face. He placed him back on the ground against a streetlight, bending Ollie's legs so that he could sit down without tipping over, making sure the poncho covered him entirely.

"Whoever lost you, they'll come lookin,'" Can Man said assuredly. Then he stood and smiled a big jack-o'-lantern smile before turning. He gave his cart a push and began to make his way down the wet, rainy street.

Ollie watched till he could no longer see him. He liked Can Man, he decided. He made him feel hopeful again.

21

TRACKS......

The Creeps were on the hunt. The Super Creep spied the dog tracks first, crossing at the exact spot where the Ollie tracks stopped. He picked at one of the imprints.

"A midsize Ruff," he determined. "Likely what the Humes call a 'Retrieve Err.'" He could see the trail quite clearly as it veered from the grass to the curb and then down the asphalt of the street. "Follow the Pup!" he shouted.

The very same Creeps who had stolen Ollie were the Creeps

most in trouble for his escape, and since they knew his world better than the other Creeps, they were in charge of tracking him. They had a small army with them, perhaps fifty Creeps in all. They scurried along the trail of the dog that had snapped up Ollie. The rain and the storm didn't bother them at all, for they enjoyed few things more than tracking a runaway Fave.

They hadn't lost one yet.

22

a pal can

As he sat hunched under his new poncho, Ollie worried. He worried that if Billy came out looking for him like that Can Man said he would, he'd get in trouble. Billy's parents were really strict about going out in the rain during a thunderstorm. And if Billy was looking for him, he prob'ly had to do it in secret, and if he did it in secret, that meant running away. And that was really, really, really illegal. At the same time, Ollie wanted to be found. *I wanna tell Billy all my huge A-venture secret scary Dark Carnival Tunnel of Lost Toys*

Danger Kid crime wave stuff, he was thinking when his thoughts were interrupted by a light metallic tapping sound coming from behind the streetlight. He looked over, and there stood a tin can hitting itself rather purposefully against the metal base of the pole. It was obviously trying to get Ollie's attention.

"Were you hiding from the Can Man?" asked Ollie.

The can bent slightly at the middle and back up again, as if nodding.

"I guess that makes sense," said Ollie, "if you don't want to get smushed."

The can nodded again, making a crumply sound as it bent. *This is a can who could be a friend,* Ollie thought. At that very instant the clatter of a thousand bits of metal rose up over the gentle drumming of the rain. The can began to shake. Ollie glanced around; he knew it had to be the Creeps. What else could it be? He spun back to the can.

"Can I call you 'Tinny'? I think we need to toddle, Tinny!" he said urgently. Tinny twonked the metal pull tab on his top and motioned for Ollie to follow him.

They bounded into the bushes and began their escape.

Ollie glanced back quickly to see how close the Creeps were. They were too close—they were already swarming around the base of the lamppost. Super Creep was circling past, his tiny headlamp flicking this way and that as he examined the trail of the Can Man.

"Which way? Whichy way is the plush?" the Super Creep asked, giggling. Creeps galore, all equipped with tiny lamps or flashlights, scanned every crevice of the curb and street nearby.

Tinny, being nearly weightless, could move much faster than Ollie. He was able to bounce and tumble and roll through yards and between houses and over fences with a dexterity that the soggy, weighted-down Ollie could only envy. But Tinny urged

Ollie on with unfailing patience, twonking his can top whenever Ollie's energy began to flag.

"Sorry, Tinny, I was pretty good at escaping before I got squishy," Ollie huffed. They managed to stay ahead of the Creeps, but not by much. By now, Ollie's poncho was torn and tattered; it hung like a pathetic Halloween costume. He was so splattered with mud, so flecked with bits of grass and thorny sticks that he was nearly unrecognizable.

This, however, proved to be useful camouflage. More than once, he and Tinny easily hid while a pack of Creeps ran right past them, for by this time Ollie looked more like a clump of muddy trash than a toy.

Finally, the rain all but stopped. And the wind quit blowing. The thunder and lightning seemed farther away but still too close not to startle. The air had an eerie stillness to it. Every sound Ollie and Tinny made seemed as loud as the snap of a firecracker.

Ollie just hoped that the Creeps weren't gaining on them.

It was during an in-between-thunderclaps quiet time that Ollie thought he heard something familiar. A sad sound. Like crying. He wasn't sure, but it seemed to be coming from under the big pointy hat boy statue thing. Even with his ears clogged with mud, there was something in the whimper that was unmistakable.

"Billy!" Ollie gasped, stumbling forward. As he did, the grass and weeds underneath the boy statue began to sparkle with tiny lights. Ollie froze. Was it the Creeps? He slipped down to his knees in the slick mud of what appeared to be an old road. No, those weren't Creeps. Those were fireflies. Tinny bounced along beside him, not making a sound. The whimpering quieted with the rhythmic blinking of the tiny firefly lights. Now Ollie could see that it *was* Billy; he recognized his backpack.

"Billy!" he shouted, getting back up and running as best as he could toward his boy, but the mud was so deep and dense.

Billy peered out from under the statue. He tried to turn on his flashlight light saber. It flickered to life for just long enough. The light fanned out and found Ollie almost instantly.

"It's me, Billy!" cried the toy. But then everything went crazy. There was thunder and lightning, and Ollie was knocked down, and the fireflies scattered, and all Ollie could hear was Billy screaming, "No! No! No!" as the Creep army overwhelmed them.

23
The junkyard of forgotten friends

It had been a ghastly and horrifying attack. And it had happened so fast. Billy had seen Ollie and was yelling like he didn't even know that Ollie was his favorite. Then Ollie was grabbed by more Creeps than he could count—they were laughing and screeching like crazy evil babies. Then suddenly, Ollie was jerked so hard, he thought his eyes would pop off. And he was tumbling, over and over in the air. He spiraled over a bank of bushes and then down into a ditch, deep in the trees.

That was where Ollie lay now, floating facedown in the rush of water that swelled the ditch because of the storm. He drifted along, occasionally bumping up against a rock or a branch, which made him bob and shift.

Billy had thrown him. Why? Why would his boy throw him away? It was a question that overwhelmed Ollie. His toy mind couldn't find a way to make sense of it, and so he stopped thinking altogether. He stopped thinking, and drifted, drifted, until he washed onto the muddy banks of an old junkyard.

A junkyard is a sad but wondrous place, a place of memories and times long gone, filled with pieces and parts of lives that have moved on. And when these broken and forgotten things are tossed away, they become junk. And they end up here—in this yard as they call it, this yard of junk.

Sometimes junk can be an old rocking chair whose cushions are threadbare from being sat on so often, whose arms have

snapped from being leaned on again and again, whose runners are worn thin from rocking generations of babies and sick children in the middle of the night.

Junk can be a banged-up old trumpet that used to play dulcet melodies but somehow got separated from its owner.

Junk can be an old typewriter used by a writer for years and years, and when the typewriter was found in the attic after the writer died, it was thrown out because almost nobody uses type-writers anymore.

Junk can be a thing called a Victrola—a beautifully carved wooden box that magically played music long before anybody ever dreamed about listening to song on devices small enough to fit in the palm of a hand.

This is where Ollie had ended up—with things broken, forgotten, tossed away. He lay there on the shore, so bloated with water, not only couldn't he move, he looked more like a wad of wet socks than a toy. This small muddy bank of land seemed the last place in the world where Ollie would ever be found.

But found he was, by four unlikely allies: Lefty, a left-handed work glove that walked on its worn fingers; Topper, a bottle opener with a sharp metal blade and a double handle that acted as legs as it teetered along; Reeler, an old, battered fishing reel that had plenty of line still twined on it, and finally, Brushes, an old, fraying paintbrush with lots of energy.

Junkyard junk looked after its own. And so it was with the Junkyard Gang. They always welcomed newcomers to this final home. After a bit of cautious observation, they determined that this soggy mass of stitchery was not a simple tangle of socks, but a toy in need of help.

Ollie dangled limply from the fishing line as they reeled him up away from the water. They hung him by the comfort of their campfire in a cove of junk at the edge of the yard. Taking off his tattered poncho, they began untangling his arms and legs, trying to wake him up. But Ollie just slumped, his head down, not a sign of life coming from him.

Ollie, however, was awake. Sort of. He heard things, but his mind was so numb, he didn't feel anything yet. He knew he was ashore. And wet. And had been found. But he felt forgotten.

Forgotten was a nothing way to feel. Forgotten was what had happened to the toys at Zozo's. And now it was happening to Ollie.

As he sat drying among this Junkyard Gang, he felt the nothing of forgotten so deeply that he didn't know how to talk anymore.

As they waited for the newcomer to dry out, the Junkyard Gang sat around the fire and told one another stories of the day when they were used, when they "belonged to."

The JUNKYARD GANG

CHILLY

REELER

TOPPER

BRUSHES

CLOCKeR

PeT ROCK

"I belonged to Mr. Gregory J. Johnson and his wife, Rebecca," squeaked a rocking chair. "She always sat on me. On their porch. Every day. Especially at sunset. It was lovely."

"I belonged to Randolf Everet alliwell," typed Keys, a typewriter whose *H* was broken. " e was a writer of mystery stories. e wrote a undred and fifteen stories wit me. Sometimes, I guessed t e mystery before it finis ed, w ich was very t rilling for me."

They had told these stories to each other countless times, and they knew them by heart. Yet they never tired of the tellings. It was their ritual, their way of remembering what they were and why they had been. It saved them from feeling forgotten.

"I was, ya know, a pet rock," said Pet Rock. "The kids Pam and Dirk picked me out. Which was very satisfying. Being picked. They glued the plastic eyes on me right there at the store place. I traveled a lot. Car trips, mostly. Arizona. California. The parking lot at Disneyland. Then one day they lost interest. I gathered dust for, I dunno, years. Then the mom tossed me."

Reeler the fishing reel's turn was next. He always went after Pet Rock. "The old man caught a jillion fish with me," he said. "Pike. Perch. Catfish. Trout. Bass. We caught a bass, on my oath, six feet long. Weighed a hundred and twenty-eight pounds."

The others groaned in disbelief. They always groaned in disbelief.

"No, really!" protested Reeler.

"Every time you tell that story, the fish gets bigger by a foot," said Clocker, who then wound herself up and began to tell her story. "*I* couldn't exaggerate. I had to be precise. The Templeton family relied on me for the time. For twenty-six years. I saw the kids grow up. And move away. All the comings and goings. All the holidays and sad days. Then Mr. and Mrs. Templeton became old. Then they were gone. And so was I."

Clocker's story always made the others grow quiet and thoughtful. But it was Clocker's story that brought Ollie back.

Without a word to the Junkyard Gang as they launched into their next story, he lowered himself down from the rope that held him near the warmth of the fire and picked up a shard of broken glass that lay on the ground. He moved slowly, as if still heavy with water, but he was, in fact, almost dry—just a little damp deep within his stuffing.

It wasn't until Ollie began to dig that the Junkyard Gang noticed he had roused. They quietly gathered around, wondering what he could be doing. He looked so crumpled and sad as he dragged the glass shard through the loose, mossy dirt again and again, making a gash.

Lefty spoke first. "What's your name, Plush?" he asked.

"I'm Topper," added the bottle opener. "We found you and brought you here."

"Reeled you in, as it were," Reeler said.

But Ollie did not answer. He just kept digging. Clocker gestured for the others to be quiet. She had seen so much; she understood that quiet sometimes said more than talking ever could. Then the old clock motioned for Lefty to go to the newcomer.

Lefty approached carefully, not wanting to startle the toy whose digging had become more purposeful and measured. It had an almost clock-like beat. One . . . two . . . dig . . . One . . . two . . . dig. With every downward strike of his shard-of-glass shovel, the bell in his chest would make a quiet ring.

The hole widened and deepened, and Ollie stayed focused on it and nothing else. Lefty very gently placed his thumb on Ollie's shoulder and kept it there.

The effect was almost immediate. Ollie froze, his arms dropping by his sides. His breathing sounded deep and exhausted.

Lefty stayed as still as Ollie, his finger never leaving the toy's shoulder. Finally, he quietly asked again, "What's your name, Plush?"

It took a moment, but this time there came an answer. His voice was clear, but when he said his name, it was almost as if it were a question. "Ollie?" Then he lifted his head and looked directly at Lefty. "I belong . . ." But he trailed off and looked away again.

Clocker shuffled a little closer. "The hole you're digging, Ollie— What is it for?"

Ollie raised his head once more.

"To forget," he answered. He placed his patchpaw to his chest. "To forget this." He pressed against his bell, a single faint chime sounding.

"I can take it out," he explained. "It's a pretend heart. It doesn't do anything. Not really. It's just an old bell. It's just pretend." And for a mournful moment Ollie felt a surge of hate at the idea of pretend. "It's fake! It's phony! It isn't real! It's just pretend!"

Again, Clocker knew to say nothing.

"But hearing it . . . ," Ollie went on. "I don't want to hear it anymore. If I don't hear it, then maybe I'll forget." Ollie looked into the hole. Then he looked at the others for a long time, his shoulders sagging. "I can't forget," Ollie said at last. "I guess I'll never ever be able to."

They were junk; they understood.

In the distance they could hear a frantic metallic plucking sound. *Ting! Ting! Ting!*

Ollie whirled around.

Ting! Ting! Ting! Ting!

Tinny? he wondered. Then, "TINNY!"

The little can bounced into the center of them. He was jumping up and down and ping-ponging off the different Junkyard Gang members, flicking his pull tab so feverishly he sounded like he was sending some kind of crazy Morse code.

"Ting-ta-ting-ting-ting. Ta Ta Ta Ta Ta ting-ting-ta-ting."

Ollie was superglad to see his friend, but he had no idea what Tinny was trying to tell him.

"I speak Can," said Topper. He listened closely, trying to grasp the *rat-a-tat-tat* of Tinny's message.

"W at's e saying?!" typed Keys.

"Gimme a sec. I'm trying," said Topper. "Okay. Something about a kid, a Hume named Bilky."

Bilky? "No, it's *Billy!*" Ollie corrected. "Billy! He's my kid! Is he okay, Tinny?!"

Topper grew increasingly grim as Tinny began ting-ing again. "He's in trouble," Topper said at last. "Big trouble."

"Where is he?" Ollie demanded, jumping up.

"Ting-ting-ting ting-ting-ting."

Ollie felt frantic. "What's he saying? What's he saying!"

"I'm tryin' . . . the . . . old carnival! The one that caved in!"

Topper turned to the others. "Zozo's got him," he said ominously.

"Zozo?!" they all repeated, just as ominously.

"Not good," added Pet Rock.

24
ZOZO A-GO-GO

Being captured and crammed into a burlap sack by a bunch of Little Ratty Toy Freaky Deaky Dementos had been the weirdest thing that Billy had ever even dreamed of. At least they'd finally pulled the sack off once they got him to the strange and disturbing place where they'd dragged him. This dark, damp kingdom of toys and weird little creatures was so bizarre that it actually delighted Billy as much as it frightened him.

It's like a Monster Scary Movie, he thought. *Like the Frankenstein guy, but with toys.* He'd watched several of these Monster Scary Movies without his parents' permission, which, of course, was a big deal and almost against the law. They *hadn't* told him he absolutely *couldn't* watch them, but Billy had a pretty good idea they would say "that's not age appropperable" or some long words like that.

So, instead of asking, he watched these movies "in secret." He'd watch the movies when his parents were napping or busy doing parent stuff. If he heard them coming, he would change the channel to *Barney* or something he knew they thought was good for him; then they'd leave him alone and he'd go back to the spooky thrills of werewolves and hunchbacks and their fog-enshrouded wonderlands that were more wonderful for not being in color. And though these Monster Scary Movies did, in fact, scare him, usually he sort of liked it. And he liked the monsters a lot more than the regular people in the story, which was puzzling to him.

"Monsters in black-and-white land are so cool," he'd told Ollie. Ollie agreed.

But right now was not in black and white nor was it on TV. This place was apparently real life, and Billy would have to deal with it. He was tied up with a dozen different kinds of rope and string, lying on the wet concrete floor in what he'd figured out was some creature named Zozo's workroom.

And he thought he knew where this workroom was, and thus where *he* was. The burlap sack had been easy to see through. For most of the journey, the Creeps had dragged and pushed him across the bumpy ground and through a wooded vacant lot. Billy'd been clever enough to shove his action figures, one by one, out of the hole he'd made in the burlap sack during the journey. Once they came to the overgrown entrance of a place called "the Tunnel of Love," Billy realized that he must be deeper within the Dark Carnival. He had walked on the outer edge of the carnival several times with his mom and dad, but they never explored it, which Billy had desperately wanted to do.

"It's too dangerous," his dad had told him. "Huge holes you can't see. Old rides practically falling down. The place is a menace."

"I loved it when I was a kid," his mom had said, and the way she had said it stuck in Billy's mind. He could tell that remembering the carnival made her happy and sad at the same time. And this made the Dark Carnival Place very interesting to Billy.

But he never dreamed he'd be at the carnival at night without his parents. The Creeps had lowered him into a rotting wooden boat in the shape of a giant swan and rowed it down the Tunnel of Love.

At the entrance he'd managed to shove his winged Pegasus out of the sack at the last second. The toy horse lay quiet and still in the grass and mud, his wings upstretched, the shadows covering him well. Perfect! None of the Creeps had noticed him as they trundled Billy along.

As Billy had lain in the bottom of the swan boat, he'd wondered if his trail of action figures and creatures was still there. And if perhaps he should have made his trail with the candy he'd packed. Hansel and Gretel had used crumbs. That had always bothered him. What if birds or squirrels or a dog had come along? So long, Hansel! See ya, Gretel! No, his small plastic pals seemed the best choice. And indeed they were. The Code of the Toys was unshakable, even for the tiniest of playthings. The code was simple: that a toy would always help whenever possible. Help make their child's day full of adventures, full of joy, full of comfort.

But this underground otherworld of Creeps and clowns had a different code, and Billy could feel that it was not a good or friendly one. As he was listening to the one called Super Creep talking to the Monster Toy Clown, he figured out these creatures had stolen Ollie at the Wedding. That their mission was to steal any favorite toy they knew about. But Ollie had escaped! Ollie had been so messed up from escaping that Billy almost didn't recognize him. Then a miserable thought came to Billy. *What if Ollie didn't understand why I threw him? What if he didn't know I was trying to save him from those Creeps? And if they wanted a favorite, why did they take me?*

These guys do a lot of illegal and commit A LOT of mean, thought Billy, and this made him feel big-time mad. Mad that they had taken Ollie and tried to do crummy bully stuff to him. Mad that they had done the same thing to bunches and bunches of other toys. Then he remembered a kid at the grocery store and how the kid had cried so hard and kept saying, "I lost Binky! I lost Binky!" And how that kid and the mom were looking everywhere for Binky. The kid was so sad that Billy felt sorry for her. Really sorry. Almost as sorry as he felt for the lost dog he saw one day when he was riding somewhere with his parents. They were in a whole different neighborhood, and the dog wanted to cross the street but was scared and shivering and skinny, and Billy yelled at his dad to stop the car so they could help the dog. But his dad said the dog would be fine. Billy wasn't so sure about that. And he thought that maybe grown-ups pretended too. But that grown-up pretending seemed more like lying than pretending *sometimes*. Billy *still* worried about that dog. Even though he'd only glimpsed it for a few seconds, Billy knew he would never forget it. Not even when he was superold, like fifty. Or maybe even older. He would remember that poor, skinny dog forever.

And then he thought of Ollie.

How Ollie had been wet and muddy and sad looking. Like

that dog. And it made Billy so sad he couldn't think about it for even one more second.

Billy had had to throw Ollie as far as he could so the Creeps wouldn't get him. And they hadn't found him. Billy could tell by what the Super Creep was now telling the clown thing.

"But, Boss, we looked everywhere," the Super Creep was explaining to Zozo, who glared down from his throne. "The kid tossed him! He *unfavorited* him!"

Zozo, unimpressed, leaned forward, his hands together like a steeple, his rusted face hidden in shadows. He said not a word.

The Super Creep hated these silences. He tried again.

"I'm telling you, Boss. If a toy ain't Faved, then it's nothin', right?"

Zozo leaned forward even more. The metal skeleton under his faded clothes creaked. With one hand, Zozo slowly reached for a saw-toothed gear that lay on his worktable.

An instant later, with sudden, blinding speed, he threw the gear across the room and neatly beheaded the Super Creep.

Billy's eyes went wide. "Wow!" he whispered. "He's a good thrower!"

The Super Creep's head rolled across the floor and came to rest just a few inches from Billy's face. It spun like a top and then slowed and stopped, its eyes looking at Zozo.

Billy was a little unnerved. Then the head began to speak and Billy was *a lot* unnerved!

"Okay, Boss, I get it. You really wanted the plush." The Super Creep's body was still standing. It staggered to its wayward head and began feeling around on the floor, but it could only guess where its head was. It began patting Billy's shoulder and then his cheek. "Wrong head," muttered the Super Creep's head. "Over here, doofus."

The body turned but accidentally kicked its own head—once,

twice—before catching it and placing it back on its shoulders, but upside down.

"I will get the plush, Boss, but"—the head tilted and almost fell—"but think about this, Boss. . . ." The Super Creep's head teetered and fell to the other side, but he caught it and held it at chest level, like a ball. "The kid can do something that no toy, *no favorite*—not even YOU—can do in a million years."

Zozo leaned back in his chair. The creaking sounded ominous.

The Super Creep spoke carefully and with emphasis. "The Kid is a kid. A *kid*," he began. "And only a kid can favorite a toy."

There was a long, unbearable silence.

"Boss," pleaded the Super Creep, walking over to the work-table, one hand holding his head onto his neck, the other pointing to the cobbled-together dancer doll who lay there and *had* lain there, lifeless, for more years than any of them could count. "That's why your dolly won't dance," the Super Creep concluded. "It won't ever. Not until a kid favorites it. And that's why I brought you"—with a flourish, he pointed to Billy—"a kid."

25
The CaVALRY!

Back at the junkyard, things were getting tense.

Billy's my favorite, even if I'm not his, thought Ollie. *He's in danger, and I've got to help him.* He felt this with the purity and strength that comes with having been a favorite toy. *He threw me away!* And that thought hurt him all the way past his stuffing and into whatever kind of soul a toy has.

The Junkyard Gang knew exactly what Ollie was feeling. If given a chance, any one of them would have rejoined their Humes, too! And while they knew this couldn't happen for them, now was a chance to be useful again. USEFUL! To be of use! And so they banded together—constructing themselves into the most unlikely cavalry of the cast off, the forgotten, and the brave—to help.

Other pieces of junk eagerly joined in the quest. Chilly, an empty refrigerator who had been junked the longest of anybody, had been the first to volunteer, and he was now being fitted with mismatched tires and wheelbarrows and a makeshift sail. The plan was to turn him into a method of swift transportation. A lawn mower named Clipper Greenfellow came forward. His cheerful, aristocratic manner gave the endeavor a certain what-the-heck flair. "Step back, fellow Junks. I've mowed the best lawns and putting greens from here to Hyde Park, and I'm ready to cut the Zozo riffraff down to size! My, I feel yar!" he drawled in his New England–playboy voice.

Reeler used his ample high-tension fishing line to bind Chilly and Clipper together. Topper, with a skill earned from opening tens of hundreds of bottles and cans, cut whatever needed cutting, adding the final touches that would turn Chilly from an oversize, white-enamel metal box into the first ever all-terrain mobile-junk attack vehicle.

Keys typed out last-minute instructions while Clocker reminded them that time was ticking.

Lefty, the only one with four fingers and an opposable thumb, was invaluable in grabbing what needed grabbing and in tying things together.

Brushes gave everyone a quick sweep so they'd look shipshape.

Pet Rock—well, Pet Rock sat in Chilly and waited. "It's not like I'm really made to do much," he said a little defensively. "I'm a pet rock."

When Keys clacked out the words, "Let loose the dogs of war!" a slew of volunteers rushed to join, filling Chilly to the brim, including a bowling ball named Burt; a platoon of knives, spoons, trowels, and kitchen utensils; and quite a few empty cans organized by Tinny.

Ollie stood on what was the sort-of deck of Chilly and wondered what to say to get them started. Keys supplied him with a quickly typed and perfectly historical phrase: "Damn t e torpedoes, full speed a ead."

26
The Dark Carnival
and Songs of Yore

The all-terrain mobile-junk attack vehicle was a triumph of design on the fly, and it functioned like a champion. They were at full throttle and sail, bouncing through the overgrown grass and puddles and roots with wicked, if wobbly, ease. The spirits of the Junkyard Gang were higher than they had been in longer than even Chilly could remember.

And Ollie was the captain. Billy had always been the one who steered when he and Ollie had rolled down hills in his red wagon, and Billy was the hero when they pretended flying and crashing and outer-spacing. But this time, Ollie was the hero person, and it wasn't pretending, it was *real*.

And this kind of REAL felt even stronger than pretending, and maybe even better. Which was strange. Everything in this crazy day and night had seemed bigger and outside Ollie's toy life. This was yum and scary and awesome, all at the same time. And he felt like he would never be quite the same. He just hoped he was as brave as he felt.

Tinny began to jump up and down and twonk his pop-top tab, motioning toward overgrown clusters of vines and small trees. The Dark Carnival was just ahead.

"Everybody hold on!" Ollie commanded as he led them closer. Then he called down to Clipper Greenfellow. "Slow and quiet, if you please."

"Aye, aye, Captain. Quiet as a green, and slow as a putt," replied the mower.

When Ollie had escaped from Zozo's, he'd been running so wildly that he hadn't really seen what the carnival truly looked like. It was, in fact, grimly enchanting. What at first appeared to be a row of odd-shaped trees turned out to be vine-covered portions of an old roller coaster.

They puttered quietly past the coaster and through the fantastic, moonlit shadowland of old rides. They were just barely visible among the weeds, vines, and trees that gnarled around and within the rusting metal shapes, which seemed like giant, leaf-covered creatures from a nightmare.

A thing resembling a huge wounded spider turned out to be a Ferris wheel, half of its spokes fallen out and small trees growing up from the listing, uneven cars. The merry-go-round had a ghostly emptiness to it. Many of the horses had snapped from their poles and now lay clustered and crammed into a frozen, tormented herd that whirled no more—sad, shadow-shrouded, and rotting. Some were held together only by dying ribbons of honey-suckle vines and poison oak.

The Junkyard Gang were quiet with awe as they passed the go-round. "They rest," Clocker said of the horses.

"Their time was grand, and they earned a better end than this," added Clipper Greenfellow.

The sight of these ruined creatures saddened Ollie. He'd seen pictures of merry-go-rounds in books. They looked so beautiful. The painted horses were like nothing he had ever imagined. He had always hoped he and Billy would ride on one of these amaz-ing round-and-round things.

"Ahoy there, horses!" he called as they inched past. "Is there anything we can do for you?"

The Junkyard Gang listened hard for an answer. A breeze rustled the grass and leaves, and to their great surprise, the go-round moved around just the tiniest bit. Its old metal and

timbers creaked and groaned. A thin, dry whisper drifted from the wreckage, like the sound of wood flaking into dust. "A tune . . . a tune would . . . be . . . welcome . . ." Then the go-round stilled. That whisper was so delicate, like a creature's dying breath. They had to do something.

"Who knows a song?" asked Ollie of his crew. They looked at one another. They all knew a song or two. The soda cans knew the jingles of their brands. Pet Rock knew lots of songs from being in the car, listening to the radio.

"Being a rock, of course, I'm partial to rock and roll," he admitted. Reeler knew many songs of the sea, but they were kinda "not suitable for children." Ollie knew some songs that were sort of more like nursery rhymes. But he realized they needed to make up their minds. Billy needed to be rescued.

"Clocker! Pick a song!" he urged.

Clocker knew a song. She'd heard it many times. It seemed

just right. She began to tick a tempo that was slow, like a waltz. One-two-three. One-two-three. It sounded not happy or sad, but somewhere in between. The can tops started twonking, forks and knives began clattering together. One-two-three. One-two-three. And Clocker began:

"Should auld acquaintance be forgot,

And never brought to mind?

Should auld acquaintance be forgot,

For the sake of auld lang syne . . ."

The Junkyard Gang began to sing along. They didn't know how they knew this song. It was a song that just seemed to . . . *be*. Like the seasons. Or the air. And it conjured up a feeling that was difficult to describe. It was tender, and warm, and stirred something deep inside them. And they played it for all they were worth. A weird and lovely blend of metals and wood and typewriter keys and plastic fishing line . . .

"For auld lang syne, my dear,

For auuuullllld lang syne,

We'll take a cup o' kindness yet,

For the sake of auld lang syne!!!!"

The song took hold of them, and they began to sing and play with more heart and strength than they thought they had left in them, and then, impossibly, the go-round began to slowly turn. The long-frozen ponies moved up and down just a little bit and the old calliope inside the carousel began to play along.

"And there's a hand, my trusty friend!

And here's a hand o' thine!

Let oooollllld acquaintance be forgot

For the sake of auld Lang Syne!"

The song had a power that was past explaining. But it made the carousel remember and be what it had been—a thing of beauty and music and joy. *Remembering is a powerful thing,* thought Ollie as their music played out into the night.

27
face to face

In truth, Zozo had never been this close to an actual child. At the Bonk-a-Zozo game, he was always behind the counter on his throne, separated by the ten feet of hope or disappointment that spanned the distance children had to throw a ball and bonk the Clown King.

Zozo walked in his slow, mechanical gait to Billy, who wriggled nervously on the floor. He leaned in close to Billy's face, staring at the way the dim light reflected and shined from Billy's worried-looking eyes. The eyes of a toy don't glisten quite like that. There was a scratch on Billy's cheek, gotten some time during the night's travels. Zozo picked at the scratch with a tiny crook of sharp metal he held in one hand.

"Ouch!" cried Billy. "Stop that!"

Zozo examined the scratch more closely. He poked again, but harder.

"OUCH!" yelled Billy. "That hurts!"

This seemed to interest Zozo. "He's torn," the clown said calmly. "And tearing him hurts." Unlike people, toys don't hurt when they're torn. They can rip an arm or lose a head, and it causes no pain at all. The pain a toy feels is in his soul, and that pain is always from loss. And loss is what Zozo had felt every minute of his life since the dancer had been taken from him.

"Sit him up!" Zozo commanded his Creeps. "Make him see my dancer!"

Billy felt pulling and poking from every direction. The Creeps were not very good at this job. They'd quickly attached ropes to the ceiling and were trying to hoist Billy up on his knees. The Super Creep's wayward head kept falling off, and his directions to the other Creeps grew all scrambled, depending on which direction his head landed. "UP! OVER!!! DOWN!!!! I MEAN UP!!!!"

Twice they dropped Billy, and he fell right on top of Super Creep. The first time, the Super Creep was just sorta smushed flattish. The second time, they couldn't find the Super Creep's head. He kept yelling, "I'm in here!" until his cohorts finally figured out he'd been knocked into Billy's pajama top's pocket. The very same pocket filled as it usually was with about six pieces of already chewed gum. It took three Creeps to unstick the head from the pocket. As they were trying to pry the gum off the Super Creep's face, Billy, trying to be helpful, explained, "That's where I keep my gum for later."

Zozo became furious and took command. The Super Creep's head was now stuck upside down on Billy's knee. Zozo left it there and focused on getting Billy to sit right where he wanted him to be. He ordered the Creeps to wrench and pull and tighten till Billy was sitting up with his legs under his chin, all of which pleased Zozo. But none of it pleased Billy. They'd been treating him roughly, like a toy, like one of the imprisoned toys Billy had seen tied to the wall in the other room.

And Billy was worried now. Some of the strings and wires wrapping around him were practically cutting into his skin. The ones around his wrists, which were pulled behind his back, were the worst. He could barely move his hands or arms without it hurting. But he soon realized that the strings around his ankles were looser, so loose that Billy could rub his feet together to get his socks to shift down, covering the obvious slackness.

At least he might be able to get his feet free and make a run for it. But the real problem now was with his knees up under his chin, the Super Creep's gum-smeared face was staring right at him.

"All right, kid," said the Super. "Look over at the table."

Billy did as he'd been told.

"See the Dancey Doll?"

Billy did see the doll. The dozen or so lights and lamps strewn throughout the lab were all aimed toward it. Billy was at first confused. The doll looked familiar. Then he realized why. How could this be possible? Could there have been more than one of his mom's favorite toys? Then without meaning to, he whispered the doll's name. "Nina."

Zozo had retreated to the side of his throne in the shadows, but when he heard Billy say that one word, he stepped closer. He watched Billy's expression with keen interest. Even after all this time, he remembered the look on a child's face when they picked their favorite toy, that sparkle in their eyes when they'd found "the one."

Billy just stared at the dancer doll. And stared. Zozo watched him with a sinister stillness. The Creeps looked nervously at one another. The only sound came from the creak and squeak of their anxious shifting.

The Super Creep—well, his head—was closer than anyone else to Billy, but he could tell from the look on the boy's face that something was up. He had seen skads of children up close over the years. He'd seen them happy and he'd seen them crying. He'd stolen many a Favorite, so he'd caused lots of tears. It was the best part of his job. Like bees to honey, he loved making tears. But Billy wasn't sad nor near tears. And he didn't look scared. The Super Creep was as scared as he'd ever been. His plan was not going as planned.

"What is it, kid?" he whispered, but Billy paid no attention to him.

"This boy can't favorite my dancer?!" Zozo said.

Billy finally looked away from the doll to Zozo.

"I can't," he said quietly. "I can't," he repeated, even more softly. "I can't. I can't. I can't. Not ever!"

Zozo grabbed a long slim rod of metal with a jagged piece of tin welded to one end. He pressed the sharp end against Billy's chest, close to the boy's heart.

"Sure you can, kid, please," the Super Creep pleaded. He could see the tip of the spear pressing tightly against the pocket of Billy's pajamas. "Zozo ain't kiddin' around."

It was so quiet and tense in that room that you could sense the tightening of every muscle, every spring, every metal joint and piece of fabric and even every breath. Then, drifting into all this stillness, came a distant sound . . . an echo . . . Music.

As if playing from far away, which it was. The sound of the old merry-go-round.

At first, none of them knew how to respond, or even if they were really hearing this strange old music. Not the Creeps, not the toys, not Billy, not even Zozo. But it played on. And then the clown king remembered. Nina. And the sound of her going away. The delicate chime of her bell. A sound he never thought he'd hear again. But he *had*, earlier that night. In the chest of a runaway Homemade.

"You know her name!" muttered Zozo to Billy. "The plush that ran." In the rusted and brittle workings of Zozo's memory, many pieces of his past were fitting together. "The Homemade with the bell. . . . *Your* toy . . ." Zozo's eyes glistened. "How do you know the name? Where is my Nina?"

The puzzle of Billy's expression was now clear.

Billy may have been afraid, but he didn't show it. He was

determined not to show any emotion at all. He would make his face as blank as a toy's. He would reveal nothing of the secret he now knew.

28
The Tunnel

Minutes earlier, Ollie and the Junkyard Gang, riding in the all-terrain mobile-junk attack vehicle, had come to the entrance of the Tunnel of Love. It was Pet Rock who spied Pegasus at the muddy edge of the ride's old canal.

"Toy horse with wings to aft!" shouted Pet Rock.

"Good eye! That's Billy's toy!" said Ollie. Pet Rock felt very proud; he did have only one eye, but it was nice to be complimented for it. "Take us aft if you please, Mr. Greenfellow," Ollie

ordered. The lawn mower promptly pulled them to the water's edge, trimming a nice path in the grass as he went.

Tinny and Lefty scampered down to retrieve the small horse and brought it to Ollie. The toy sensed the naval spirit of the mission and reported thus:

"Pegasus reporting for duty, sir!"

"Tell us what you can, Pegasus!" said Ollie.

"Well, Captain," the toy replied, recognizing Ollie's leadership role. "The hostiles brought President Billy to this point and then smuggled him aboard a large wooden swan and sailed the swan down the canal and out of sight."

President Billy? That sounded right. To a kid's toys, their child does seem like a president.

Tinny and Lefty looked up to Ollie for direction. Ollie sensed his crew had confidence in him, and that gave him a surge of braveness. So much braveness that it scared him, because Ollie knew they didn't have a plan. Ollie had been Billy's second in command for many pretend attacks and invasions, and he kind of knew the words to say, like "Charge!" and "Cover me!" and "Use the Force Luke!," but he had never imagined that he would ever be leading a real mission. Yet here he was.

A real boy—his boy, President Billy—was captured by real bad guys. Guys who did so much illegal and mean and cruddy that Ollie'd have to be the bravest and best Grand High Safemaster of any kid ever in all of history. He had to do this for Billy, even if Billy had chucked him away. It was the Code of the Toys. And this kind of Real was a little scary. Actually, this kind of Real was REAL scary.

Ollie stared down into the dark, watery tunnel. They all did.

"Man, it's dark in there," said Topper.

"Really dark," agreed Reeler.

"So dark I couldn't see my thumb in front of my palm," said Lefty.

Tinny had followed the Creeps into the tunnel when they Billynapped Billy, and even he couldn't help but shake a little at the thought of going back. And his shaking made the other cans shake. And then the knives and forks were shaking. Then Keys started typing lots of question marks. And the music from the merry-go-round started sounding kind of spooky in the breeze. And now, the all-terrain mobile-junk attack vehicle was rattling and clattering so loud. You could actually hear their fear.

What do I do?! Ollie thought. Even his own bell was ringing! *I'm not made of brave. I'm just . . . stuff!* But he KNEW what he had to do. He had to find Billy.

The breeze calmed, and the merry-go-round sounded less strange, and then, at the entrance of the tunnel, tiny dots of light began to appear. First, a dozen or so. Then more and more.

Fireflies! Hundreds of them, some drifting all around them, but more gathering around Ollie, so many it was almost blinding. "I think they're here to help us," said Ollie. And though the Junkyard Gang could barely see Ollie for all the flickering, they weren't afraid anymore: they all knew that there was nothing to fear from fireflies. Then the little glowing insects began to drift away, away from Ollie, and back toward the tunnel. They darted into the dark entrance, lighting it up. Just enough. Just enough that Ollie and the others could see. See what was ahead.

29
The Canal

Ollie thought of every trick he'd ever seen in every battle movie he and Billy had watched and in every book that had been read to them. "Okay!" he commanded. "Our plan is gonna be: do some Robin Hood, and some Use the Force Luke, and some Trojan Horse, and some . . . Yellow Submarine."

The Junk kinda understood. Luckily, Chilly was watertight when closed and could submerge like a submarine. His ancient cooling motor would act as a perfect propeller to power the refrigerator at a good clip through the thick, murky water. Once inside Chilly, the platoon of tin cans had been busy arming themselves with wheels and arming themselves with knives and forks and ingenious little bows and arrows made from every kind of scrap imaginable. So on Ollie's order, Chilly submerged.

Ollie told Pegasus to guard the tunnel entrance while he and the rest of the Junkyard Gang leaped into one of the wooden swan boats bobbing in the water. They pushed themselves away from shore and let the swan drift into the tunnel, just ahead of Chilly. They hunkered down and hid. Every piece of Junk knew what they were supposed to do in a general sort of way. They were cocked and ready. Locked and loaded. Full of vim and vigor. Swash and buckled. And lots of other hero phrases they weren't sure they understood. The fireflies continued to hover above them, but as they neared the end of the ride, the insects began to

go dark. Ollie, peeking past the swan's long neck, could see that the dock at the other end was unguarded, and—could it be? Yes! It could!—just beyond that was the room of the lost toys. Ollie could hear voices. One was definitely Zozo's and the other . . . Billy's!

Ollie turned to his crew. "Okay, everybody! You know what to do!" he whispered.

"Pretty much!" "Kinda!" "I think so!" came their replies.

"Not so loud, guys," hushed Ollie. "Remember, this is a super-spy, super-sneak-up, super-ninja-man, surprise attack-the-bad-guys super attack."

"Yeeeeeeeeeeeeeeeeeeeaaaaahhhhh," they all whispered back, feeling super-spy-inner-ninja non-Junkiness filling their every molecule.

Ollie waited patiently till the swan finally nudged up against the edge of the decrepit old dock, which was literally the end of the ride. He spoke quietly into a walkie-talkie. "Tinny, can you read me? Tinny, come in!"

After a moment there came *"Ting! Ta ta ting."*

"Good," replied Ollie. "Tell Chilly to remain submerged till I give the order. Do you read me?"

"Ta ta ta ting."

"Okay, hang loose," said Ollie. He peered carefully around. A single firefly drifted forward, as if making sure the coast was clear. It hovered near the top of the door that led to the lost toys' prison room, then blinked several times.

"That must be their signal! Come on!" Ollie waved the gang onward, and they began to slip and climb and spring and tiptoe from the swan boat to the dock and then toward the entrance of the lost toys' prison. The room was dim, the only light coming from Zozo's lair.

"Can we yell 'charge' now?" asked Pet Rock.

"No," said Lefty. "We're still sneaking!"

"Well, can we yell *sneaking!*, then?"

"I don't think so," said Topper.

"I think we just sneak till it's officially charge time," added Brushes.

Keys was being pushed along by several Junk helpers, and Clocker was riding along. Everyone had an old steak or butter knife, or a bent fork or a fondue spear as a weapon, except for Pet Rock—he really couldn't hold anything. "Just throw me! Hard! I'm a rock! I can take it!" he insisted adamantly.

Ollie was the first to reach the forgotten favorites' door, and through their prison, he could see into the well-lit chamber of Zozo's lair and across the room to Billy. There was Billy!

Billy was sitting up with his knees to his chest and his back toward them. Several dozen Creeps surrounded him—the room was lousy with Creeps. And there, just past Billy, was Zozo's table.

And on the table was a doll, a ballerina doll. It looked like— No, it couldn't be. But yes, it did—it looked just like the Nina doll from that photo of Billy's mom from long ago. And standing next to the doll was Zozo, looking intently at Billy.

30
the Echo

Ollie inched forward. He was not walking like a regular plush; he was walking like a plush on a mission! The rest of the Junks followed his lead: attentive and at the ready and very, very surprise attacky.

They sneaked past the imprisoned lost favorites who recognized Ollie and understood immediately that they were not to make a sound. Some of the toys looked more tattered than they had when Ollie first met them. After they'd helped him escape, the Creeps and Zozo had clearly not been gentle. Some of them were nearly torn to shreds. One-Eye. Carrot Bunny. Dino. They had all lost some fabric or stuffing or parts. But they didn't mind. As soon as Ollie and his crew began to untie the them, they immediately fell into rank, eager to help.

Once they were all free, Ollie edged himself up against the wall just beside the door of Zozo's lair. He could hear Zozo easily now, and what he heard was alarming.

"This boy can't favorite my dancer!" Zozo was shouting.

"I can't," Billy said quietly. "I can't," he repeated, even more softly. "I can't. I can't. I can't. Not ever!"

Ollie snuck a look. Zozo was placing a sort of spear against Billy's chest.

Then things went quiet. Ollie glanced back at the gang, worried.

"Now!" whispered Pet Rock.

Ollie shook his head—no—urgently. He wasn't sure. He knew deep down inside that he had to wait for something, but he wasn't sure what. He was feeling so many things at once—scared, brave, calm, and something else. Something mysterious. Like a memory he didn't know he had. He was waiting. He looked up. The fireflies were clustering again, just above him, their lights very dim. Then the brightest one buzzed down and landed on his chest, just above his bell heart. As Ollie watched in surprise, the firefly blinked on and off, on and off. Blink-blink . . . Blink-blink . . . like a beating heart.

As the firefly continued its blinking rhythm, Ollie understood what the firefly was trying to tell him. His bell. His heart. It had been more than just his—it had been Nina's before him.

Blink-blink, blink-blink.

He knew that at that same moment, Zozo was pushing his

spear against Billy's chest, just above Billy's heart.

Zozo's voice boomed. "You know my dancer, don't you! I can tell from your face. YOU KNOW HER! HOW?"

The firefly stopped blinking. And Ollie knew what to do. He began to pound his chest as hard as he could, making his bell ring loud and clear.

31
CHARGE !!!

Billy eyed Zozo. "I'm sorry, Mr. Zozo," he said with calm defiance. "But you're right, I can't favorite your Nina. I already have a favorite, and his name is Ollie."

The sound of the bell had transfixed Zozo. "My Nina. My Nina," he said almost tenderly. Then his face made the closest thing to a smile the Creeps had ever seen Zozo make.

Billy knew this was his chance. Ever so slowly, so no one would notice, he reached down to knee level and pressed one hand over the Super Creep's mouth. Then he started sawing his wrist bindings against the sharp edge of the Creep's tin-can head. He was nearly finished when there came a funny sort of shout, not of a person, not of a child or even an animal. It was the unmistakable cry of a toy. A very brave and valiant toy. *His* toy.

"CHARGE!!" bellowed Ollie.

Then every piece of Junk and every ancient toy joined him in a great magnificent roar, "CHAAAAAAAARRRRRRGE!!"

And they charged.

The Creeps were too stunned to react. Before they could put up their guard, the Junks and toys were overrunning them, swatting the first wave of villains down like flies.

Billy jerked around, an openmouthed grin of surprise on his face. He spotted Ollie rushing forward, taking the lead, sword slashing left and right so fast that no Creep in his path stood a chance. They were actually running AWAY from him.

252

"Look at him go," Billy murmured in happy, bewildered awe.

It took Billy an instant or two to absorb the fact that Ollie was leading a charge.

In those few seconds, the Creeps had regained their senses and started to fight back with their usual skill and cunning. But not before a protective blockade of junkyard warriors and determined toys surrounded Billy. "President Billy!" cheered the Junks.

"Stay in formation until I can get him free!!!" Ollie shouted, leaping up to Billy's knees and stepping on the Super Creep's gum-smeared head.

"Yikes!" said Ollie.

"Back atcha," replied the Super Creep.

"'President Billy'?"

"It's been a weird night," said Ollie. Then he slashed at the last threads of Billy's wrist bindings with his sword and cut right through them.

"Wow," said Billy. "You're a good battler, Ollie!"

"Thanks, Billy," said Ollie, feeling kind of proud and glad and super relieved, all at the same time. And Billy felt the same way.

"I thought I was gonna rescue YOU!"

"Well, I learned how to from YOU," Ollie answered as he yanked away the last of Billy's bindings. There was no time for hugs or slobbers or any of that stuff. There was a battle going on.

"Now, let's get out of here!" Ollie ordered.

"Ditto," Billy agreed, hopping up, shaking the bonds from his legs. But first, there was something he needed to do. Because he was mad now, mad at Zozo for all the illegal and means he'd done. He wanted to find that clown toy. But Zozo was nowhere to be found.

Billy saw Ollie looking at the dancer doll on Zozo's work-table.

"It's almost exactly like Mom's," Billy said.

Ollie nodded.

"I bet Mom misses her. The way I'd miss you. I'm gonna bring her home to Mom!"

Then Ollie knew what *he* had to do.

For the first time, Ollie didn't agree. In every game, or huge A-venture, or just goofing around, Billy had always been the leader. But things had to be different this time.

"No, Billy," Ollie said—not in a mean way or in a fun way, but in a sort of older-sounding way.

"Huh?"

"We can't take her," said Ollie. "She belongs to Zozo."

"But she looks just like Mom's Nina. . . ."

"But she's not your mom's Nina. Your mom loved her Nina to

pieces in long, long olden days ago. It wouldn't be the same," said Ollie.

Billy thought about that. He knew there could only ever be one Ollie. But before he could agree, a sudden, alarming jerk and sway rippled through the room, followed by a sharp rhythmic crackle of breaking concrete, as if a giant hammer was pounding upon the tunnel floor. The lamps began to swing in different directions. Then the back wall of the chamber crumbled down, filling the room with rubble and dust.

Junks and Creeps alike scattered as concrete and bricks tumbled toward them.

Billy scooped Ollie up.

Out of the clearing haze crept a terrifying, crab-like multi-legged machine, taller than a man, with the legs made of mismatched girders and pieces of old carnival rides. At its center was an old bumper car, painted with a smiling face—the kind of cheerfully hideous face you only find at carnivals. And there, behind its steering wheel, sat Zozo, the clown king, his face grue-somely lit by the dingy flashing carney bulbs that pocked the machine. A single scorpion-like tail, attached to the back, coiled and struck through the air.

"Uh-oh!" said Pet Rock, who had been thrown during the thick of battle by Lefty and was now on the floor, right beside Ollie and Billy. "I think this might be a good time to shout the run-away word."

Ollie couldn't agree more. "RETREAT!" he commanded, though he needn't have, as everyone was already retreating as fast as they could. Billy spied Pet Rock and grabbed him.

"Thank you, Mr. President," said Pet Rock.

Ollie turned on his walkie-talkie and yelled instructions to Tinny. "Surface Chilly! Send in the cans! We're escaping!"

Zozo struck at them with the scorpion tail. Ollie and Billy

darted out of the way. The tail struck a wall behind them, and it began to crumble down. Billy and Ollie dashed toward the docks.

Zozo and his machine were close on their heels, knocking down walls and smashing through doorways that were too small. The Creeps swarmed right along with him, like an army of crazed spiders.

"Does retreating mean we aren't brave anymore?" shouted Lefty, holding Keys while Clipper Greenfellow soared full speed toward safety.

As the Junks and toys scrabbled onto the dock of the Tunnel of Love, however, there was no sign of Chilly.

"Uh-oh!" Ollie looked anxiously from the swan boat to the surface of the water. "There's not enough room on the swan boat for everybody."

But at that instant, Chilly breached the surface like a giant cork, sending water splashing up as if a bomb had gone off.

"Hooray!" yelled Junk and toys alike. As Chilly settled, his door swung open and out sprang Tinny and his brigade of cans. And not a moment too soon, for the Creeps were spilling down toward them, determined to halt the escape.

Ollie shouted. "Tinny! You gotta hold 'em till we get the old toys aboard."

Tinny and his cans—armed with their bows, spears, and swords—made a protective line, three cans deep, while Ollie and the rest of the Junkyard Gang helped the toys evacuate.

Once most were onboard, Ollie commanded, "Now, aim Keys toward the door!" The Junkyard Gang knew exactly what to do and were at the ready to feed the typewriter with an endless supply of tacks that would fire like Gatling guns from his keys.

The Creeps made a formidable mass of cheerful wickedness and were actually singing a gruesome sort of war chant, banging their weapons against their metal shields or chests or whatever part of them would make noise.

"Slash! Cut! Tear the toys up!

Off with the arms!

Off with the legs!

Off with the toys' little bitty heads!"

Meanwhile, the last of the old toys were being hurried toward the swan boat. And Billy heard some sort of mutiny taking place.

"I want to fight!" said One-Eye Teddy, who appeared to be leading a group of teddy bears who refused to be evacuated. "We, of the League of the Bears of Teddy, demand the right to fight!" he yelled. He turned to Billy. "Mr. President! You have executive powers. Grant us a pardon. Let us do our duty!"

Billy had to remind himself of the little bit of history he knew about teddy bears. They were invented way back in horse times in honor of a real president of the US of America named Teddy Roosevelt, who was a soldier who went up a hill to fetch a pail of water or something, and there was a big fight, and so teddy bears were invented, and Billy thought they must be sort of soldiery too.

"Okay, teddies!" Billy agreed. "Get with the cans!"

"Yes, Mr. President!" They all saluted smartly and then joined the line. Billy saluted back. The battle was about to begin, and he needed a weapon. Then he spied it.

In the great clutter of carnival odds and ends that was scattered around the Tunnel of Love dock lay a flagpole from one of the old attractions. It wasn't long, but it was long enough. And the tattered flag affixed to it was simple. Just one word, or rather, a name, was emblazoned across it: ZOZO. And on the end of the pole was a carefully carved head of a clown, its peaked hat making a sort of spear point. Billy snatched it up.

Meanwhile, Zozo's mechanical monster, too big to fit through the doorway to the docks, began pounding the doorframe, its scorpion-like tail smashing the supports around it.

Then came a terrible, deafening crash. The walls around the door collapsed, and in crawled Zozo on his awful machine. The chanting Creeps let out a fearsome cheer, and they made ready to attack.

Billy gripped his pole-spear tightly. Then—*yeowwwch!*—something bit him on the ankle. Hard. He looked down. The Super Creep's head was caught on his sock! It must have fallen there during all the craziness. Billy yanked it off and brought the battered head to eye level.

"You gotta stop Zozo, kid," the Super Creep said, his voice raspy. "He'll tear up everybody. He don't care about anything but his hurt and hate."

Billy was just tucking the poor Super Creep's head into his pocket, about to reply, when Ollie broke past Tinny's cans. Yelling "Charge!" once more, he plunged all by himself, toward Zozo and his army.

32
the fireflies of TRUTH

In an instant, Zozo struck, and this time his aim was true. He hit Ollie, pinning him to the ground. Ollie struggled to sit up, but the front legs of Zozo's machine pressed heavily upon him. Then the machine kneeled, bringing Zozo eye to eye with the struggling toy. Its scorpion-like tail arced menacingly, poised to strike again, its sharp point ready to rip Ollie to shreds. The Creeps, shrieking joyfully, ran pell-mell toward Billy and the ragtag army of toys and Junk.

"Let 'em have it!" shouted Billy. And the Junkyard Army made the air thick with tacks and arrows and pieces of pointy junk. It was a withering barrage.

The first line of Creeps crumbled like dried leaves, but the next wave sped forward, hitting the line of Tinny's cans like a landslide.

Keys let fly with thousands of tacks, typing a jillion words a minute, faster than any human, while the Junkyard Gang kept up the steady stream of pointy projectiles as if they'd been battling danger their entire lives. The tacks pierced the Creeps with such force and accuracy, they could barely advance. They were knocked to pieces or pinned to the floor or one another, becoming a comical clot, a staggering mass of Creeps and clutter and uselessness.

Billy rushed forward to help Ollie. The teddy bears, like crazed Cossacks, followed close behind, thrusting aside every Creep that Keys hadn't crippled. It was a battle royal! A chaos of forks and

cans and toys and Creeps, slashing and fighting and tearing away at each other till the whole room became a blur.

A great many things happened in the next few seconds. Time seemed to slow down as the fates of many were decided.

Zozo was wild with hate. He could not stop himself. For Zozo had only one thought: the Homemade must die. He let the scorpion-like tail strike.

And strike it did.

But it did not hit its mark.

At the last instant, Billy lunged, and with a speed he did not know he possessed, he blocked the deadly tip of the machine's tail with the flagpole. The tip hit the pole's carved clown's head, splitting the head nearly in half. It could go no farther.

33
Remembering

Ollie was sure he was dead. He just couldn't figure why there was a small wooden Zozo head directly above him, with the tip of the scorpion tail between its eyes. He turned and saw Billy stood next to him, holding a spear thing. On its end was the splintered wooden Zozo head.

Then he looked over and saw Zozo, the real Zozo, in his monster machine. But Zozo wasn't looking at him, he was looking up. And so was Billy. Ollie's gaze shifted to the same direction.

It was the fireflies. More fireflies then he had ever seen. Thousands of them. Brighter than he thought possible. They were swirling, coming together into a sort of shape. A familiar shape.

Ollie scooted out from beneath the pierced spear. As he stood, the battle came to a halt. Everyone was transfixed by the sight of the fireflies.

The fireflies drifted closer and closer together until the shape they were forming grew unmistakable. It was the face of Nina the dancer doll, but as a thousand blinking points of light. Their glow filled the dock with a strangely comforting wax and wane of light.

And from it came a voice, a voice almost chime-like. Nina's voice.

"Stop, Zozo. There is no need for worse," she said. "These toys have done you no wrong."

Zozo said nothing.

"I never forgot you, Zozo," the dancer doll continued. "I was your favorite and you were mine. But I became a favorite to a child and lived a long and generous life. And when that child loved me to pieces, I became a spirit. A guardian spirit who watched over another favorite, the toy called Ollie."

Ollie turned to face Zozo.

"I'm not your enemy, Mr. Zozo," he said.

Zozo looked grimly at Ollie, then questioningly at the vision above him. His hate continued to ebb, but he uttered not a sound.

Nina grew brighter. "He's telling you the truth, dear Zozo. The bell was mine. You remembered its sound well. It was Billy's mother who favorited me. She kept that bell and placed it in Ollie when she made him. But dolls and bells aren't enough. I could not come back to you until the hate left your heart." She grew brighter still. "Zozo," she beseeched, "you were once a king and did your best to comfort all. Remember. Remember. *Please* remember."

And at last Zozo's expression shifted. Despite the rust, despite

the flaking paint, his face softened. His eyes never leaving the vision above him, he finally spoke. He spoke softly, and kindly, in a way that had not been heard since long, long ago.

"I remember," he whispered. "I remember now."

At that, more fireflies appeared, seemingly coming from every direction, until they formed Nina in her entirety from head to toe. This Nina of light drifted over to Zozo and cupped his face with her hands.

And in this miraculous light, Zozo's face grew less fierce and frightened as the decades-old hate dissolved. "I remember," he whispered again with a tenderness that was unexpected. "I remember." And this moment seemed endless, outside of time. Each of them, even the creepiest Creeps, felt a strange peace as Zozo and Nina remembered.

And everyone waited.

Waited to see what would come next. What came next was a

snap—the loud snap of breaking concrete—and the room quaked like doom. No longer able to take the strain of the missing walls, the ceiling began to sag.

"It's going to collapse!" cried Topper.

A massive chunk of ceiling began to give way. In a moment everyone would be crushed. Because of Zozo. Because of his hate. Long, long ago, he had been unable to help his toy friends. He would not let that happen again.

He raised his machine's legs, as well as the scorpion's tail, until they reached the sagging ceiling and braced against it.

"Go!" he commanded, sounding like the king he once was. "Hurry!"

Billy grasped Ollie by the ears and he, along with the last of the toys, the Junks, and even the Creeps scrambled onto the swan boat and Chilly. Another section of ceiling fell, but Zozo used all his machine's legs and tail to keep the ceiling from caving in. The last of them scrambled onto the swan boat and Chilly, and just as the ceilings, the walls—everything—began to crumble, Zozo used one leg to shove the boats off and down the canal.

Billy held Ollie close as they looked back to see the room cave in completely. The fireflies were gone—and so was the glowing Nina.

So was Zozo.

Buried.

But once again . . . a king.

34
"Good-bye" is not so good

There is a strange quiet after a great struggle.

The swan boat was ashore outside the Tunnel of Love. Chilly was back on his wheels, and reattached to Clipper Greenfellow. As they stood there, they each knew that their lives would be different somehow. Friendships had been made, great journeys taken, battles fought and won, enemies were now allies. Billy stood looking at the confusion all around him. Talking gloves and paintbrushes, ancient toy warrior spoons . . . It was hard to get used to. Ollie was sitting on his shoulder and could tell Billy was shivering a little as he picked up Pegasus from the grass.

"I guess we'll have to find a new word for all of this," said Ollie.

"It was a real adventure," said Billy.

"Not A-venture?"

"Nope. That's a little kid's word. This was an Adventure."

Ollie thought about that. He wondered if he and Billy would ever have another huge A-venture again. The wind began to pick up, and something bright in the sky caught their attention. It was the fireflies, weaving in and out until they formed two familiar shapes. One was the Nina. And the other? They weren't sure at first, and then they all knew.

"It's Zozo," whispered Elephant in awe. Every toy, Creep, and piece of Junk began to whisper his name again and again.

"Zozo." "Zozo." "Zozo."

Billy was the only one who didn't say his name. But Ollie did.

Zozo had been a toy, like him, and seeing Zozo and Nina—two glowing spirits, drifting in the wind, drifting above the trees and out of sight—moved Ollie. *Zozo has forgotten his hate and remembered*, thought Ollie as he put his hand over his chest. His heart had been on a long, long journey.

So much had happened and so many things had changed so quickly that words seemed very inadequate. For with all the change, there also came to each of them a quiet understanding:

It was time to go home.

And going home meant parting ways for this mismatched band.

So it was that the Junkyard Gang climbed aboard Chilly and readied to head back to the yard. Good-byes were new to Ollie. He'd said good-bye to some dogs at the park, but this good-bye felt like a much bigger good-bye. It felt like a good-bye for a long, long time. Or an "I don't know when I'll ever see you again" good-bye.

Or even, even, EVEN a forever good-bye. And that was something big for Ollie. It felt much bigger than those two small words.

Billy felt it too, for though he really didn't know these pieces of stuff very well, they had helped rescue him and they were Ollie's friends and even that felt strange, that Ollie had friends other than Billy. This sort of bothered him, actually. He felt a tinge of jealousy. But he pushed that feeling away and, with Ollie sitting on his shoulder, he walked up to the all-terrain mobile-junk attack vehicle.

"Thank you, guys," he said shyly.

"You're welcome, Mr. President!" the Junkyard Gang said loudly and in unison.

Billy sort of shook his head and smiled. "I'm just Billy."

"You're welcome, Mr. President I'm Just Billy!" they replied. Billy decided not to correct them again. Then came one of those times when no one knows what to say, so they don't say anything for so long that it gets all weird and uncomfortable.

Finally, Ollie jumped down from Billy's shoulder and stood among his new pals. Reeler, Topper, Clocker, Brushes, Lefty, Keys, Chilly, Clipper, Pet Rock, and Tinny gathered around him. They'd only known one another for one night, but sometimes that's enough.

"Come by the yard sometime," said Clocker.

"I will," Ollie promised. "Thank you. Thank you all for everything."

"Hey," said Pet Rock. "Thank *you*! Nobody's thrown me for ages!" That made them laugh. When the laughter stopped, Ollie smiled sadly at them. He felt a heaviness inside as he jumped back up to Billy. Good-byes in movies always had music in them that sounded like good-bye feels. There wasn't music in real life, but this good-bye felt very real. And "good-bye" was a word he didn't want to say.

He looked at Tinny. He knew he couldn't say good-bye to the

tin can that was braver than any of them. Tinny gave a slight bow, making a crinkling sound as always. Then the can sprang forward and landed with surprising accuracy into the open top of Billy's backpack. From inside, they could hear Tinny ting ting ting-ing mischievously.

"Tinny isn't really junk," said Clocker, and Ollie nodded. But he still didn't know how to say good-bye to the rest of them. He then remembered a movie where seven good guys had to fight a bunch of bad guys, and when the good guys had won, they didn't say good-bye to everybody; they said another word, and so Ollie waved one hand and said that word instead.

"*Adiós.*"

Then Clipper Greenfellow replied, "*Vaya con Dios,* old sport." Revved his motor and pulled the Junkyard Army away. Each and every one of the Junkyard Gang waved and waved. Ollie stared after them until they disappeared into the dark.

Billy had never really seen Ollie sad before, and for a moment it made him feel kinda . . . separate from his friend. They had always been together, and so they pretty much felt the same way about things. Except when Billy was sad, then Ollie would cheer him up by being funny or goofy. But Billy wasn't sure that this was a kind of sad he could fix by being funny. This was a lot worse than "skinned-knee" sad. Or "I dropped my Popsicle" sad. So Billy decided he would just say the thing that he knew they both needed to do.

"I think we should go home now, Ollie." As Ollie nodded, however, they heard a coughing sound behind them, as though someone was trying to get their attention. And then a nervous little voice spoke up.

"We want to go home too." Billy and Ollie spun around. Standing there, very patiently, were the forgotten favorites! They stared up at Billy and Ollie hopefully. Worn and faded, frayed and torn, they were the most homesick bunch of things you'd ever seen, but they had a quiet nobility to them. *They look like really old knights who've been in many battles,* thought Billy, *and they're ready to finally go home.*

"Do any of you remember where you lived?" Ollie asked. The toys shuffled around glumly.

"Not really," said One-Eye Teddy.

"Being an elephant, I should remember," added Elephant. "But I don't." They all looked down, seeming heartbroken.

Billy turned to Ollie. "We've gotta figure something out!" Ollie looked at Billy in surprise. It was the first time Billy had ever asked *him* what they should do. But before Ollie could answer, a muffled voice rose up from Billy's pocket. It was the Super Creep. Or, well, his head. Billy had completely forgotten about him. He pulled the gum-smeared little head out, and the Super Creep started talking a mile a minute.

"I remember! I remember where every one of them lived. I helped steal them all!! I'm the SUPER CREEP, am I not?!" The other Creeps drew closer.

"But we're the bad guys. We can't take 'em home," Creep 2 protested.

"Who says?" the Super Creep replied with plenty of attitude. "We've been the best bad guys around; now let's freshen up the act. Try something new. Ya know, a *real* challenge."

Creep 3 shrugged. "He's gotta point. Being good would be a BIG challenge."

"All right, it's settled." Super Creep grinned. "Now, will somebody find me a body, please. And hurry it up. We gotta lotta ground to cover."

Billy tossed the Super Creep's head down to his troops.

"Thanks, kid," the Super Creep said. "You and the Homemade did pretty good."

As the Creeps began to organize the Faves, the teddy bears came up and saluted Billy.

"It was an honor to serve you, Mr. President," said One-Eye Teddy. Billy saluted them back with a smile.

"You got a *lotta* new friends," said Ollie, half joking.

"It's okay, Ollie." Billy then made sure Ollie was hanging tight around his neck as he began to walk away. "I've only got *one* Favorite."

And as they walked out of the old carnival and toward home, the teddies began to sing "Hail to the Chief," and even the old merry-go-round joined in.

It wouldn't take Billy and Ollie long to get home. Billy had his trail of action figures to follow. And a very good song to send them on their way.

35
the trail of toys

And so they began the walk home.

"We should go patchpaw...." Ollie told Billy. "No, wait.... The other way? ... Um ..." Ollie had done many amazing things this night. He made great journeys and commanded an army the likes of which had never been seen, even in a daydream. But he realized he did not know the way home.

"It's okay, Ollie," said Billy. "I left a trail of friends to help us." He pulled Pegasus out of his pocket. "The rest of the guys are along the way."

"You're a good trail-leaver, Billy," said Ollie, and then he settled into Billy's backpack and just let the nighttime world go by. Every now and then, Billy would lean over and pluck up another action figure guy (and three warrior princesses) as they got closer to home. There was so much to talk about and tell, but they could do that later.

The walk home was very different from any they had ever taken before. And, in fact, Billy and Ollie were different now too. It wasn't a different you could see, though they surely looked different—both were astoundingly dirty, covered with dust, grass stains, and smears of mud. Ollie even had a few tiny arrows stuck in his fabric.

But they were mostly different *inside*. And in ways they couldn't quite grasp. They could just barely see the park gates when Ollie said:

"Should we tell Mom about Nina and Zozo?"

Billy thought about that for a moment and finally said, "No . . . she'd . . . just freak out or something."

"Then you can just say that you went looking for me, and I was right where you left me."

Billy laughed a little. Ollie knew there'd be a lot more questions if they were caught sneaking back home. But he was too tired to come up with any more ideas. Besides, Billy was probably right. Grown-ups liked questions, but they didn't seem to like answers nearly as much.

"Man, we did A LOT of brave tonight, Billy," he said.

"Yeah, and faced A LOT of bummer, and crummy . . ."

"And fought A LOT of mean and got STORMED on . . ."

"And had a battle royal!"

"And *saved each other's day!*"

Then Billy stopped. He leaned over and picked up Grongo, the Twig Man of Planet Zaxxo. He handed the little plastic alien to Ollie. "He's the last one."

"Good job, Grongo," Ollie whispered to the toy as he tucked him into the backpack. They were almost home!

"We saved A LOT of people's day," Billy reflected in a far-away voice, and they both thought about the Junkyard Gang and the forgotten toys and the Creeps and then even Zozo and Nina.

"Ya know, Ollie, there's a lot of nutty stuff out in the world," said the muddy, tired boy, sounding almost wise. "Bummer and bliss out. Scary and safe. All at the SAME time."

Ollie completely agreed. But he also felt a tinge of unease— Billy, his Billy, almost sounded like a grown-up. *Almost.* So he snuggled up against Tinny and tried not to think about it. Billy walked them out the park entrance. He looked both ways and crossed the street without even thinking it was a big deal. They saw flashing lights. Lots of them. Police cars were PARKED

RIGHT IN FRONT OF BILLY'S HOUSE!

"Wow," said Ollie. "I think we're going to jail!"

"And the lock key is getting thrown *far* away."

36
at a threshold

Coming home was very strange. There were a lot of police cars and a lot of lights going flash flash flash across the lawn and the house and the policemen and -women who were staring at Billy and Ollie as they walked into the yard.

"We surrender!" said Billy, putting his hands up. "We crossed a lot of streets without permission. . . ."

Then Billy's mom came running down the porch faster than Billy had ever seen any mom run. And she was in her pajamas and robe! In front of people!

She reached out and practically knocked Billy over as she picked him up and hugged him tight. So tight.

"Billy! Billy! Billy!" she kept saying in a funny crying sort of way. She was hugging so hard that Ollie was getting squeezed out of the backpack. She ran with Billy in her arms across the lawn and up the steps to the house.

Ollie asked Billy, "So are we in trouble?"

"I'm not sure," Billy whispered from within his mother's crushing hug. And as she ran through the open front doorway, Ollie fell out of Billy's backpack and landed on the floor of the entrance.

Ollie sat there on the threshold. Not inside or out, but in between. The stillness of dawn seemed to quiet the sounds of the fading night. The thunders, winds, and roiling leaves, all the shouts and cries and songs, seemed now to have been a very vivid dream. He couldn't see Billy or his mom; they were down the hall in the TV room where Billy's dad and the police people seemed to be talking all at once. Ollie wasn't really hearing them.

He was sitting there and wondering about everything. He wondered about Can Man, and the lost favorites and his junkyard friends. He wondered about Zozo and Nina. But mostly he was wondering about the future. He knew that everything would change. He knew that Billy would grow up. Pretending couldn't stop that. Can Man's face was what comforted him the most. Can Man's look of remembering. Remembering. "Remembering" was a word that made Ollie feel *real*. It didn't matter if something was pretend or real; if it was remembered, then it was true. If it was remembered, then it didn't go away.

"Remember" is a good word.

Ollie knew this now.

Billy would always remember.

And Ollie would never forget.

As he sat there, he heard footsteps coming toward him from down the hall. But it was dark inside. He hoped it was Billy. And he waited for the next part of his long Aventure to begin.